THE BIG TREE

Rick Hautala

First Edition

ISBN: 1-938644-10-7
ISBN-13: 978-1-938644-10-8

Nightscape Press, LLP
http://www.nightscapepress.com

FOREWORD

Rick didn't talk a lot about Rockport—not in the way that some people do about their hometowns—but occasionally he would reminisce about his childhood there, about swimming in the quarry with his friends or the relationships he had with his parents and siblings. So it came as a surprise to me when I learned that, in the aftermath of his death, his wife Holly discovered a memoir among his papers. Rick had written this autobiography in 2009 and then promptly deleted it from his computer files, but he had left a hard copy behind. I relished every page of that manuscript. It was like a wonderful, final conversation with Rick, during which I learned more about his youth—and about his career—than I had ever known before.

Then, immediately after I finished reading that memoir, I received an advance copy of *The Big Tree*. What a pleasant surprise to find that this story, one of Rick's final pieces of fiction, is suffused with the same sense of nostalgia, the same innocence and sadness and strange wonder, as his personal autobiography. For me, the beauty of this piece is that there is so much of my friend in these pages. Rick played a significant role in my life for more than two decades, so it was wonderful to hear his voice speaking to me in *The Big Tree*.

It will be a different experience for readers who did not know Rick personally, and yet I have no doubt that the raw emotion he conveys will come through loud and clear. There's a veracity here, in the midst of this story about a deadly hurricane and a lonely boy and a lost girl who is much more than she seems. Writing is something like acting. Character is a mask the author wears. But sometimes the actor—the author—is able to tap something much deeper and his or her own true self shines through. In the dread and awe of *The Big Tree*'s young protagonist, in his wonder and curiosity so beautifully conveyed and his yearning for understanding, you will meet Rick Hautala's true self.

What a gift.

—Christopher Golden

ONE

Ever since I can remember, all of my friends and I called it simply the "Big Tree." It was a huge oak tree that stood back from the road in the Wayrenen's front yard, next door to the house where I grew up. I could see it from my bedroom window.

Whenever any of us neighborhood kids wanted to meet up, all we had to say was, "Meet me at the Big Tree," at such-and-such time, and we'd be there. In so many ways that I didn't really appreciate until much later, the Big Tree was *the* center of our neighborhood.

What happened after it blew down in 1960 during Hurricane Donna certainly changed my life. I'm still not sure if it was for better or worse.

Of course, back when I was a kid, Old Lady Wayrenen didn't like us climbing and playing around in the Big Tree. Whenever she caught us up in its branches, she'd yell at us to get out of there or else she'd call our parents.

She was old. I thought she was as ancient as the oak tree in her front yard. We knew she would never

1

come outside, and even if she did, we were too fast. We could easily outrun her. The worst she could do was complain to her son, Walt, who would tell us to clear out.

Walt knew we'd always come back. He was an "old guy," too—I figure in his thirties—but from my perspective at the time, I remember thinking that he must remember what it was like to be a kid because he was always laughing at us and seldom got angry unless we were goofing around in his horse barn and spooking the horses. We knew Walt didn't really care if we climbed around in the tree like chimpanzees. Whenever he came around, we would make it a game to hide in the foliage as high up as we dared climb so he wouldn't see us. We never got caught, but I suspect he knew exactly where we were, and he simply let us be kids.

Old Lady Wayrenen's grandson, Jimmy, was my best friend... at least until we started high school. Then we drifted apart. That summer of the hurricane, he told us that his "Mu-mu" had taken a turn for the worse over the winter. She couldn't even get out of bed any more, and Walt and his brother, John—Jimmy's father—took turns bringing her meals and coming to visit. Everyone called Jimmy's father "Jussi," his Finnish name. She'd still yell at us when she heard us outside, but we never saw her at the door or in the window anymore. If Jimmy was telling the truth, she was yelling at us from the bed her sons had set up for her in the living room.

I'd never actually been inside Old Lady Wayrenen's house, but from time to time I'd peek inside while I waited outside on the granite doorstep for Jimmy. He stayed with his grandmother a lot. I found out later it was because his father and mother weren't getting along very well. They got divorced three or four years later.

"Don't you think she'd like hearing us out here playing and laughing?" I said one fine, warm afternoon as we were lolling around on the lower branches, trying to stay cool and figure out what to do.

It was early September. School had started on Tuesday, the day after Labor Day. The weather was way too hot for baseball, much less touch football at the park. We might have gone swimming at Steel Derrick, the granite quarry where we usually went, but we were still at an age when an adult, usually one of our parents, had to go with us... like we were little babies or something. My dad was always too busy working to take us anywhere, but Jimmy's father went with us sometimes. Lately he'd been working with his brother, doing masonry work, so we were stuck.

Jimmy jumped and waved a deer fly away from his face.

"My Gram don't like us out here 'cause," he said, "'cause it reminds her she's getting old and is gonna die soon."

Now there's a thought—I couldn't help but shudder in spite of the heat—*knowing you're going to die soon...*

It sure scared the crap outta *me*.

Sure, I was young and healthy, if not exactly a tough guy, like Phil Balzarini and "The Twins," George and Ralph Sweet. They were the neighborhood bullies, at least as far as I was concerned. Those three were always threatening to beat up me or one of my friends. Usually they didn't do anything, but every now and then they'd follow through with their threats, and I'd been at the receiving end of their fists a few times. Mostly, though, we avoided them, and they stayed clear of us, preferring to hang out together and smoke cigarettes and—I don't know—probably torture small animals. Jimmy always said they were too busy jerking each other off to bother with us, but that was the kind of talk that, if it got back to them, would get you pounded.

Speaking of scared, though, Jimmy had expressed to me and our friends plenty of times how much his grandmother scared the bejeezus out of him. My clearest memory of her is that voice. I'll never forget it. Even now that she's long dead and gone, I can still hear her cracked, shaky voice, wailing from the dark rectangle of her living room window, yelling at us kids, telling us to "Get out of that tree or I'll call your parents!" I always pictured her as a withered old hag, but of course now I realize she was nothing more than a feeble old woman who was dying—probably of cancer—and deserved pity more than anything else.

But back then, we didn't have the sense to pity anything. There was no way we were going to give up hanging around in the Big Tree.

We couldn't.

The Big Tree was *ours*, not hers or any other adult's.

Even Phil and the Twins stayed away, although once we built our tree house about fifteen or twenty feet up, we always wondered who swiped three of the copies of *Playboy* we had stashed up there. I always thought it might have been Ray, another one of my friends. He was always complaining about how the pages were getting soggy. Maybe he decided to keep them in the privacy of his bedroom. But he and

4

Jimmy and Jimmy's younger brother, Chucky, all insisted Phil and The Twins had taken them. After that, I kept a few older copies up there, but I hid the newer issues under a stack of boxes in the back of my bedroom closet. They were safe there until I went off to college. When I came home for Thanksgiving my freshman year, the *Playboys* were gone. Maybe Bobby had taken them, but I assumed my mother had found them and thrown them out. I certainly wasn't going to ask her about them.

"So whatdayah wanna do?" Jimmy asked.

"I dunno."

I could tell he was just as bored as I was. Every year, by the end of the summer, I was glad to be back in the routine of school, even on the weekends, we were bored a lot of the time... at least we said we were. There were lots of times when I preferred to be alone in the Big Tree. Sometimes... a lot of times... when my friends were off somewhere else and my brother was bugging the crap out of me, usually insisting it was my turn to mow or rake the lawn or clean our bedroom, whatever, I would climb up into the highest branches as high as I dared to be alone. Jimmy always went higher, but that was Jimmy.

Sometimes I'd perch on a branch and read, and sometimes I'd just sit and look around at the narrow confines of my world and talk to myself.

I've heard later in life that talking to yourself is a sign of insecurity, and that may very well be true. I wasn't the happiest kid going, that's for sure. I'm not sure why. Looking back, I assume it was just the way I was wired. But I had a lot on my mind—doing homework, being bullied by my brother, trying—often without success—not to get into trouble, and having thoughts and feelings about girls—especially Sue Crowell—that intrigued and confused me.

There was nothing wrong with me or my family that I could see. As my mother always said, "Be thankful. You have everything you need, and nothing you don't." Sure, my older brother was a bully, but whose older brother wasn't? And maybe my dad didn't spend much time—that is, any time—with me. We never went to ball games at Fenway Park; he never even came to my Little League games. He never took me fishing or anything. I can remember one family vacation when I was a kid, other than the two weeks my brother and I got shipped off to summer camp. But I didn't fault my dad. It was because he was always working. He worked for the town as the water engineer, and evenings and weekends, he was working his part-time job as a land surveyor.

So until I was in high school and had a summer job, I was pretty much left to my own devices, and I usually ended up high in the branches of the Big Tree where I talked—muttered, is more like it—about the things that were bothering me. I unburdened myself in a low, whispered voice that, I imagined, matched the voice of the tree talking back to me in a whispery flutter of leaves or the faint creaking of branches as they moved gently in the wind.

The Big Tree knew all of my secrets.

I was an imaginative kid, no doubt, but I knew in my heart that the Big Tree couldn't actually *hear* what I said, much less feel what I was feeling. I had a lot of feelings I couldn't begin to express. Maybe that's why I eventually became a writer—to get some of that stuff out. But when I couldn't concentrate on what I was reading—usually a *Tarzan* book, loaned to me by my teacher, Mr. Ives—I would talk to the Big Tree and tell it how sad and lonely and at times frustrated I was that my life wasn't turning out the way I imagined it would. Of course, if anyone had asked me to describe how I thought my life should be, I would have been stumped. But sometimes I tried mightily to convince myself that the wind whispering through the leaves and the steady creaking of the swaying branches were answers... if only I understood the language.

"You hear the news?" Jimmy asked.

I shook my head.

"What news?"

"On TV."

My father and mother watched the evening news, but all I ever saw were scary stories about how the Soviets were going to blow us up with A-bombs if we didn't blow them up first.

"There's a storm coming," Jimmy said.

"A storm?"

"Uh-huh. They're saying we might get hit by a hurricane."

As soon as he said the word *hurricane*, my stomach froze like I'd just swallowed a handful of crushed ice. We'd had some big storms before that I remembered, especially in the winter, but a hurricane?

"Aren't they like tornadoes that tear houses down and stuff?"

"I heard my parents talking about it, and—yeah, they can be wicked bad."

"When's it coming?" I asked, hoping my trembling voice didn't betray my sudden flood of worry. Ever since I was little, I remember being fearful that I would lose my family home because of a fire or something. One Christmas Eve, I ended up crying because I was so afraid the Christmas tree would catch fire and burn the house down. Even today, I make double sure the tree lights are unplugged before I go to bed.

But a hurricane?

"They're saying it's gonna be here the first of the week—Monday morning and last probably into Tuesday."

"Jeesh, really?" was all I could say.

"I hope we get it wicked bad." Jimmy said. He craned his neck and looked up at me, a big grin spread across his tanned face. His blue eyes looked as pale and cold as ice cubes. "That way they'd have to cancel school."

"I guess so," I said, but there was a hollowness in my voice because all I could think about was that this storm was going to be really scary... maybe even horrible.

And it was, but in ways I never could have imagined.

TWO

By Sunday, everyone was talking about Hurricane Donna. At church that morning, people were as talkative and friendly as ever, but many of them had a kind of worried look in their eyes. The minister, Pastor Sarvala, even asked in his prayer that God would spare us the worst of it. He also mentioned the damage the hurricane had caused further down south, and how people had been flooded out of their homes or had them crushed by falling trees.

Like I said, I'd always been a worrywart, but now I was scared. If the minister was asking God for help, we were in for it.

After lunch, I hung out with Jimmy and Ray the rest of the day. I got to the tree house first, so I read some of my *Tarzan* book until they came. After goofing around some, we went into the tree house and flipped through the well-thumbed pages of my *Playboys*. We didn't talk about the knockers on the women, though. All we talked about was the coming storm.

There was a definite calm… a weird stillness in

the air like I had never experienced before. A hush, like the whole world was waiting for something to happen. Even the birds seemed to know something bad was on its way because they weren't singing like they usually did.

"This is really creepy," I said, shifting my eyes back and forth between my two best friends. I wondered if I could tell them how afraid I was and if they would admit the same.

"I know," Ray said. Beneath his summer tan, his face was pale.

We all jumped when we heard a cowbell ringing, the signal Ray's mother gave when it was time for him to come home for supper. We could always hear the cowbell, even when we were playing deep in the woods, but for some reason, today it sounded like Mrs. Makkinen was right there in the tree house, ringing it.

"Ahh, man. I gotta go," Ray said, looking despondent.

"When you gotta go, you gotta go," Jimmy said. "Speaking of, I gotta take a leak."

He squeezed out through the rough-edge door onto the narrow landing before Ray or I followed. I took the time to hide the *Playboys* in case anyone else—especially a parent—ever came up here. I heard a loud thump when Jimmy vaulted up onto the tree house roof. I was crawling through the door when I remembered that I'd left my *Tarzan* book up there. I called out, "Hey! Watch out for my book!"

Standing with his back to us, Jimmy zipped his fly down and began to pee. The only sound in the hushed silence was the splattering as it sprinkled onto the leaves and branches.

"Don't get any on my book, you jerk," I shouted when he started twisting back and forth, spraying the branches. The cowbell was still clattering away, and before he started down to the ground, Ray cupped his hands to his mouth and, leaning his head back, shouted as loud as he could, "Coming!" Smiling back at us, he said, "Probably see you guys tomorrow, then, huh? 'Specially if there's no school."

"I guess so," I said with a tight smile and a nod, but all I could think was Jimmy'd tried to piss on my book. He never did like to read.

If the coming storm was as bad as everyone was saying, then we might not see each other ever again... We might all be dead by tomorrow evening.

"Catch' yah later," Jimmy said, turning to face me as he zipped up his pants. I caught a glimpse of his weenie and was surprised to see how big it was. It had to be at least twice as long as mine.

Ray clambered down to the lower branches and then, leaning down and grabbing one near the ground, swung out into the air. He kicked and let out a loud *whoop* before landing on the ground with a dull thud. His mother was still ringing the cowbell, and he shouted again that he was coming. This time, apparently she heard him because the ringing suddenly stopped. He picked up his bike from the ground where he'd left it and, holding the handlebars, started running beside it until he had enough speed to swing up onto the seat. His bike chain rattled as he pedaled over the bumpy ground down to the street.

"See yah!" he called out over his shoulder, and then he was pedaling furiously down the street.

Jimmy climbed down to the ground while I went and got my *Tarzan* book from the tree house roof. My stomach tightened the instant I saw five or six drops of pee that had splattered on it, discoloring the faded red cloth cover. My first thought was that Mr. Ives would never lend me another book if I returned this one ruined. I was shaking inside as I dropped from a branch down to the ground, landing right next to Jimmy.

Without a word, I clenched my fist and punched him—hard—on the biceps.

"Ahh, Jesus! What was that for?"

He was rubbing his upper arm as I showed him the wet spots on the back of the book. He narrowed his eyes and shook his head.

"What's your problem?"

"You pissed on my book. That's what!"

Before he could duck or back away, I pressed the wet side of the book against his shoulder and wiped it down his shirt. It left a long wet streak on the book cover, but I hoped it would dry soon enough. I'd leave it in the sun for a while, but it grossed me out to think that Jimmy's piss was on the book I'd be holding in my hands to read tonight.

"Why do you have to be such a jerk," Jimmy said.

"Why do you?"

He didn't say anything more as he walked away, massaging his arm where I had hit him.

"*I'm* not the jerk," I shouted to his back. "*You're* the jerk."

He kept walking until he got to his bike. Tears were shimmering in his eyes when he picked up his bike and looked back at me.

Suddenly I wanted to say something... that I was sorry... that it was no big deal, but I was still mad. I was convinced he had tried to pee on my book, but even if he hadn't... even if it had been an accident, he should have known better. Only then did I realize he might feel bad about not thinking it through before doing it.

"You going home?" I asked, my voice tight. I wanted to part as friends.

Without another word, Jimmy swung his leg over the bike seat, settled his right foot on the pedal, then kicked off. His shoulders hunched up like two narrow blades beneath his stained, white t-shirt as he rode away. I was left standing there, and all I could think was—if I was right, and we all ended up dead from the hurricane, I was going to be *r-e-a-l-l-y* sorry that I'd been so mean to my best friend just before we all died.

THREE

As evening—and the storm—approached, the world began to feel really weird. There was an uncanny stillness. Maybe you've experienced it at some point in your life… what they call "the calm before the storm." One thing I noticed this time, though, was that it wasn't small and personal, not at all like the anxiety I experienced waiting for Christmas morning to tear into my presents or the day of a big test at school when I was convinced I hadn't studied nearly as hard as I should have.

No, this was definitely different.

This was way bigger than those things.

It was the kind of feeling that happens only when something beyond anyone's control is about to happen.

Even back then, I remember wondering if that eerie feeling was as much in my head as it was real.

For one thing, the strange stillness that settled over the land made it feel as though the air had suddenly gotten much thinner. I wondered if maybe that was really what a hurricane did. I scared myself, thinking: *What if the storm is so big it punches a hole in the upper atmosphere, and all our oxygen is sucked up into space?*

The leaves of the Big Tree were perfectly still, not a breath of air to stir them. The upper branches above the tree house were drooping, hanging lower than usual. I had the crazy notion that the tree knew what was coming and was hunching its shoulders, preparing for the blows to come… just like I did when I knew my brother was about to punch me. As daylight faded and the clouds moved in, the overcast sky had a weird bruised purple glow that removed all shadows. The sound of the crickets chirring in the Wayrenen's horse field on the other side of my house was unusually loud, like they were the only things in creation not filled with foreboding.

I was afraid. I wanted to talk to someone about it… like my mother. I wanted to tell her what I was feeling and ask if we were going to be all right, but all of the adults in the neighborhood—my parents included—were busy putting stuff away and tying things down. At the horse barn behind our yard, Jimmy's uncle Walt nailed boards across the stall doors to keep them shut while Jimmy's father, Jussi, drove the tractor, bringing the last of this year's hay bales into the barn. Jimmy and his brother Chucky helped by pitching the hay bales up into the loft, but all I could think was the barn was going to get flattened by the high winds headed our way.

My dad used a tow chain with links the size of my fist to tie the picnic table to one of the birch trees close to our back porch. If he was afraid the table might blow away, we were definitely in for it. That thing was huge and must have weighed at least a hundred pounds. My mother took the clothes off the clothes line. She always washed our bed sheets on Sunday and air dried them. I loved the fresh smell they got. The pinched expression on her face bothered me to no end, and I was afraid to go to her for consolation because I had no idea what I'd do if she told me she was just as scared as I was.

I felt helpless... absolutely useless, like Bobby was always telling me I was.

Before supper, I had asked my father again what I could do to help. He told me he had everything under control, so I went into the house and asked my mother. She had already put the laundry away and, before she made the beds, was searching through the cupboard for candles and batteries for the flashlights. Her only suggestion was to go upstairs and fill the bathtub with water so we could use it to flush the toilet if we had to. That seemed like an unimportant thing to do, but I went upstairs and did it anyway.

That evening at supper, we all seemed to try too hard to talk about anything else. For me, that only made it worse, especially when my brother started teasing me, saying I looked so scared, like I was going to pee my pants. My father told him to knock it off, but Bobby was a persistent tease and kept making fun of how nervous I was.

After supper, I offered to help my mom wash dishes. She expressed surprise, and asked why I was being so helpful. I mumbled something lame because I didn't want to tell her I wanted as clean a conscience as possible if I was going to die tonight.

Once the supper dishes were done, we watched TV for a while. My mother and father sat on the couch. My brother took the easy chair, and I lay flat on my stomach, facing the TV, my chin propped in the palms of my hands. As usual, my brother and I argued over whether we should watch *Dennis the Menace* or *Maverick*, but I won—one of the few times I remember ever winning an argument with him—because *Maverick* was on from 7:30 to 8:30, and my mother always watched *The Ed Sullivan Show*, which started at 8:00. When my dad told us to go to bed after *Ed Sullivan*, Bobby contended there was no way we'd have school in the morning, why not let us stay up a little later. But my dad insisted, so up the stairs we trudged.

Even after I washed up and tucked myself into bed, my nerves were on edge. I felt like there was something vibrating inside me... like the tuning fork Mrs. Jacobson, our music teacher, showed us last year. I closed my eyes and listened for the hum but heard nothing. Even with the lights out, there was no way I would get to sleep. I had my bed by the window, so I propped myself up on a couple of pillows and, folding my arms to rest my chin on, leaned on the windowsill and stared out at the darkness in the yard.

I have always liked sleeping near an open window, even in the winter, although my brother complained and threatened to punch me if I didn't close it. That night, with the window opened wide, I inhaled the damp night air and listened to the hush that was wrapped around the world. By now the sky was overcast. I couldn't see any stars or even the moon.

"You think it's gonna be as bad as everyone says?" I asked Bobby. He was lying in his bed on the opposite side of the room with his back to me. Like

18

usual.

Shut up was Bobby's usual response to anything I said, so I was surprised when he said, "I sure hope so."

"What d'yah mean?" I asked, trying not to think about how dangerous the approaching storm was going to be.

"It'll be great. A day off from school. Trees and power lines and all sorts of crap will be down. Maybe even some houses. When it's over, me and Johnny and Roy are gonna go around the neighborhood 'n ask people to hire us to help 'em clean up their yards. We're gonna make a *ton* of money."

That sounded like a good enough idea, and I felt a twist of guilt for not being so ambitious, but all I could think about was how trees and houses—maybe even *our* house—might get flattened by the storm.

"Now shut your mouth and go to sleep," he said.

That was more like him.

I didn't say a word as I turned my attention to the view outside the window. Off to my left was the huge, black bulk of the Big Tree. It towered against the sky, looking like a giant splash of ink against the dusky night. I stared at it so long and so intently that my eyes began to play tricks on me. Whenever I shifted them a little bit left or right, I imagined I saw what looked like a person moving about on the lower branches, below the tree house. It was hard to see because everything was so dark, but the longer I stared at the Big Tree, the more distinct the figure became.

I had learned a trick long ago about seeing things in the dark. If I shifted my gaze a little to one side or the other, then I could see what was directly in front of me more clearly. I asked Mr. Perry, our science teacher, about it. He said it had to do with how our eyes are made. I'd have to look it up to explain it now, but it had something to do with the cones and rods in our eyes, the parts that can see in the dark. I tried shifting my vision like that now to see if there really was someone out there.

"Can't be," I whispered out loud, and then I cringed, waiting for Bobby tell me to shut up.

Maybe it was Jimmy or another one of my friends.

Maybe one of them had decided to ride out the storm in the tree house so he could brag about it.

Maybe, I thought, but if one of them was going to do that, he would have told me, I was sure.

Well, Jimmy might not have if he was still mad at me for punching him so hard. While he was working with his brother, getting some bales of hay into the loft, I had waved to him, but he didn't wave back. I told myself it was because he hadn't seen me, but honestly, I knew he was still mad at me.

I shuddered at the thought of being up in the Big Tree… alone… on a night like this.

If one of my friends really was up there, he was braver—or crazier—than I was. The few times we had tried to sleep out in the tree house, we ended up coming back inside for one reason or another… usually because one—or all of us—got scared, although we'd never admit it. Sometimes, especially in the summer when we camped out in a tent in the backyard, my friends and I would sneak out and run around the neighborhood, raising a little hell. We'd peek into lighted windows or raid neighbors' gardens to help ourselves to fresh corn on the cob and tomatoes and cucumbers. Stuff like that. Sometimes we'd even walk all the way into town, about three miles away, but I didn't do that very often. I was always afraid someone would recognize me. They'd tell my folks, for sure. Any sleep-outs would be out of the question for the rest of the summer if not the rest of my life.

But I was sure there was no way Jimmy or any other friend of mine would be out there in the Big Tree tonight.

My eyes must be playing tricks on me, I decided, but that didn't stop me from staring at the Big Tree or still seeing a shadowy figure flit back and forth among the branches.

I have no idea what time it was when it started to rain. I was so entranced watching the approaching storm that I didn't bother to glance at the alarm clock on the table beside my bed. I stayed right where I was, chin resting on my forearm, shifting from time to time when I got uncomfortable as I stared out at the world and inhaled the damp, earthy smell that wafted to me when the wind gradually rose. Something unimaginably big and dangerous coming our way got steadily stronger, but it was taking too long. I was impatient for the storm to come blasting into the area if only to relieve the dreadful feeling of impending doom. Throughout my life, I always preferred to deal with something straight on, no matter how horrible, rather than sit there and wait for it.

But this storm was coming, and there was no escape… not for me or for anyone, including someone I think I came to love.

FOUR

At some point during the night, I settled down in my bed. The next time I woke, it must have been close to dawn because the sky wasn't entirely pitch-black. The wind was blowing harder now, and rain sprayed in through my open window, moistening my face and pillow. For a panicky moment or two, I was confused about where I was. The walls and ceiling and everything I could see around me—which wasn't much in the eerie half-light—seemed unfamiliar.

"Shut the window," my brother muttered in the dark. His voice sounded like his mouth was full of sand. I wondered if he was awake or talking in his sleep.

But I did what he said because my bed and I were already wet. The window chattered in the frame as I pulled it down. Then, once my head cleared, I realized where I was and what was happening.

The hurricane was finally here.

I glanced at the clock by my bed and saw that it was a little after four.

It was too early for my folks to be up unless, like me, they were worried about the storm. I listened to see if I could hear my dad snoring like he always did in their bedroom downstairs, but I couldn't hear a thing above the sustained roar of the wind and the muffled pounding pulse in my ears.

The storm filled me with inexpressible awe. I sat there on my bed, listening and watching as the trees waved wildly back and forth. Leaves and small branches were blowing everywhere. Already, our lawn and the driveway were covered with drifts of fallen leaves. It was going to be one heck of a cleanup, I could see that.

The rain came in fitful blasts that splattered against the window like buckshot… stopped… and then came again. The icy sound set my teeth on edge, but I couldn't help but wonder what it would be like to be out there.

"And this is only the start," I whispered to myself.

My breath fogged the window glass, and I stared into the eyes of my dim reflection. I got the unnerving sensation I was looking into someone else's eyes. I didn't know what the word *dissociation* meant then, but I do now.

Once the idea of going outside was planted in my brain, I couldn't get rid of it. I wanted to feel the force of the wind and rain. Looking over at Bobby's dark, rounded shape, I had no doubt what he would do if I woke him up. He'd probably squeal to my parents about what I was doing… or else punch me out.

Moving slowly, I got out of bed and started to get dressed. Tension filled my belly as I thought how I was actually doing this. It was stupid… maybe dangerous, I knew, but I had to do it.

What if a tree fell on me and killed me… or the wind was so strong it carried me away?

But a spirit of adventure enveloped me and overcame my worries.

Tossing the bedcovers aside, I slid quietly out of bed. When my feet hit the floor, a loose floorboard beside my bed made a loud snap that made me jump. I froze, thinking it was loud enough to wake up everyone in the house. It was certainly loud enough even with the wind howling under the eaves and roaring through the trees. I waited for my brother to react, but he kept on sleeping.

Moving as slowly and quietly as I could, I took the jeans I wore yesterday from the chair where I had draped them last night and slipped into them. I picked up yesterday's dirty socks, which I hadn't tossed into the laundry yet, and pulled them on. They were crusty with dirt and dried sweat, but I figured I was going to be so wet they'd get washed while I was wearing them. After lacing up my sneakers, I tiptoed over to the door and was out of the room.

Everything was good so far, but I still had to get downstairs, through the living room and dining room and kitchen, and out the door without my parents catching me. The spirit of adventure and the danger of getting caught made the skin on the back of my neck tighten as I started down the steps. It was dark in the stairwell, and I slid my right hand along the wooden banister to help me keep my balance. It seemed as though every step creaked beneath my weight, echoing in the stairwell much louder than normal.

At the foot of the stairs, I paused and looked around the darkened living room. I half-expected to see my mother or father sitting on the couch, waiting for me to realize they were there. The storm hissed and blew outside, but the stillness in the house was uncanny.

The clenching feeling in my gut almost sent me scurrying back upstairs and into bed, but I took a deep breath and walked on. Now that I had started this foolish adventure, at the very least I was going to have to open the back door and step outside onto the porch so I could at least say I experienced the raw power of nature unleashed.

I made my way slowly through the dining room and kitchen until I came to what we called the "utility room." This was a one story addition on the side of the house. The roof was right outside my bedroom window. The washing machine and dryer were there along with a long, narrow table where my mother kept some house plants. There were two doors, one leading out to the front steps, the other opening onto the back porch. I called it a porch, but it was really a wide cement platform without a roof.

To one side of the front door, there was a row of pegs where we hung our jackets and sweaters and, in the winter, our heavier coats. I fumbled around until my fingers grazed the slick back of a raincoat. I couldn't tell whose it was. It felt bigger than mine, so I guessed it was either Bobby's or my father's. The jacket made a loud ripping sound when I zipped it up. Then, still walking on tiptoes, I walked over to the back door. My hands were clammy and shaking as I reached for the doorknob. We never locked our doors at night. The doorknob clicked softly when I turned it. Before I opened it, though, I sensed something behind me. A tiny squeak came from somewhere in the back of my throat as I turned and looked to see who—if anyone—was there. The wind outside howled so loud now I couldn't have heard anyone if they were sneaking up behind me. Staring into the darkness of the kitchen, I imagined I could see a dark figure flitting about, but I realized it was only an illusion created by the streetlight shining through the waving branches of the tree out in the front yard.

You don't have to do this, a voice whispered deep inside my head.

I knew I could choose to not do it, but that was the problem. It would be chickening out. I wanted to go outside and feel the full power of the storm. When I looked outside, though, I had serious second thoughts. The wind blew the rain almost horizontally. Already, the backyard was littered with leaves and broken branches. The birch trees where my mother had her clothesline were thrashing back and forth like snapping whips. I could see my mom's clothesline was broken. It lay like a thin, gray snake across the grass.

Still telling myself I was crazy to be doing this, I turned the knob and pulled the door open. Gusts of wind banged like drumbeats against the screen door. I hesitated, but only because I was afraid the louder sound might wake my parents.

There was no sign they were up, so I triggered the latch on the screen door. As soon as I pushed it open, the wind ripped it from my grip. It swung on its hinges and slammed against the side of the house like a firecracker going off close to my head. I was amazed it hadn't been torn off its hinges. As I stepped out onto the back porch, a solid wall of wind and rain slammed into me. I felt like I'd been hit by a truck, and I was positive I wasn't going to get the screen door closed. It would end up slamming back and forth

27

against the side of the house until someone—probably my father—woke up and came outside to see what was wrong.

But—somehow—I managed to pull it shut without breaking it. The wind whistled shrilly through the wire mesh, setting my teeth on edge. But that was nothing compared to the full force of the wind that seemed to vacuum my breath out of my lung in a single whoosh. I had to cover my face with my hands before I could take a deep enough breath.

I looked up, wincing as rain pelted my face like a steady blast of BBs until I turned my back to protect myself from the full brunt of it. My hands shook wildly as I tugged the hood up over my head and pulled the drawstrings tight so there was just a small, round opening I could look out of. The splattering sound of the rain on the rubber coat was loud, reminding me of sitting in a pup tent when a sudden cloud burst opens up.

All right, I thought… *now what?*

I was out in the storm, so what was I going to do?

The wind buffeted me from all sides, knocking me around like I was being pushed by invisible hands. The wind fanned water from the roof in scalloped sheets, spraying the porch. A loud, low-throated roar almost below the level of hearing filled the air. It sounded spooky and gave me goose bumps. I heard another, higher-pitched sound and realized it was the telephone wires, humming in the wind like someone wildly strumming on guitar strings.

I considered walking over to the Wayrenen's horse barn and seeing what—if any—damage was going on there. Rain was rushing down the barn's steeply pitched roof, sending thick, silver sheets twisting away in a wild spray. I wondered how the horses were doing, but I decided not to risk going over there. If they were spooked or something bad happened and they broke out of their stalls or out of the barn, I didn't want to get blamed for it.

Still shielding my face with both hands, I turned to my left and looked out across the side yard toward the Big Tree. I couldn't believe what I was seeing. Even the lowest branches, which always seemed so strong and stable, swayed heavily up and down and side to side. They made low creaking sounds like they were shattering inside from the strain. The upper branches whipped and snapped back and forth. Cascades of leaves blew away with every powerful gust as if huge, invisible hands were stripping them away.

Through the waving branches, I caught glimpses of the dark blocky bulk of our tree house. The rain-soaked boards were as black as oil. The bulk of it that seemed so sturdy when my friends and I sat in it was bouncing up and down like a boat tossing about in rough seas. I imagined the nails holding our tree house together slowly, inexorably pulling free. Maybe—even as I was watching—the boards would blow away and clatter down the street like tumbling dice. Convinced the tree house was going to be smashed to splinters any second now, I coiled my body, preparing to leap off the porch and run over to it. I stopped myself. If it was going to go, it was going to go, *Playboys* and all.

There was nothing I could do to save it.

As I watched the tree bend and heave from side to side, I thought I saw something else.

The rain was blowing so hard it shifted gauzy curtain between me and the Big Tree, and through the wind-tossed branches and blowing leaves, I was positive I saw a dark shape skittering up and down the branches independent of the waving motion of the tree.

Even though I knew it was impossible, *someone* was climbing around in the Big Tree.

I was sure all my friends were safe in their homes… at least as safe as anyone could be in a storm like this. There was always the chance that a tree could come crashing down on someone's roof. But if it wasn't any of my friends, who or what was it?

What if a hobo, maybe one of the old drunks from down on the wharves had gotten it into his head that he could weather the storm in my tree house?

Maybe he had gone up there to steal my copies of *Playboy* and now, drunk as a skunk, was climbing around in the branches like he was a sailor scampering up and down ratlines on the mast of a sailing ship. My friends and I sometimes pretended the Big Tree was a clipper ship, so why not some old drunken fisherman?

I quickly dismissed that idea, though.

It would have been beyond crazy for someone— even a drunk bum—to climb into the Big Tree in weather like this

In the end, I convinced myself it had to be a trick of the eye… an illusion created by the dense darkness of the storm, the tossing branches, and my own rational—and irrational—fears. If my brother knew what I was thinking, he would have teased me mercilessly… like always.

The wind and rain battered against me. A few gusts almost blew me off the porch, and I had to grab the edge of the doorjamb to hang on. I knew I should go back inside, but I couldn't look away from the Big

Tree.

"There's something there," I whispered even as the wind stuffed my words back down my throat.

I jumped when, in the corner of my eye, a sudden dark blur moved behind the door window. My heart leaped into my throat, and I let out a high, bleating cry when a face suddenly appeared. It took me a frozen second or two to recognize my father. He glared at me through the glass like I'd lost my mind. In a way, I guess I had. He threw the inside door open, and I stepped back and opened the screen door. The wind all but tore it from my grip. It slammed into the side of the house, leaving a fresh gash in the shingles.

"What the devil are you doing?" He had to shout so I could hear him above the wind. He reached past me and yanked the screen door shut. The wind through the screen whistled shrilly.

"Just… checking it out," I said humbly as I pushed past him into the safety of the house. When he closed the door behind me, the sudden concussion of silence stunned me. The wind and rain still beat against the house, but it sounded impossibly far away after being out in the full force of it.

"Stay on the rug," my father said, pointing to the floor. "Your mother will have a cow if you get her floor dirty."

"It's just water. It'll be—" I started to say but then shut up when I saw the look on my father's face. There was no arguing with my dad—*ever!*—so standing on the rug, I carefully shed the raincoat, making sure the drips—at least most of them—landed on the rug. I didn't dare ask what he thought my mother would say about me getting her throw rug soaked. No way was I going to ask.

My jeans from the knees down were so saturated they felt as heavy as leg irons around my ankles.

"Might wanna take your pants off, too," my dad said.

The washer and dryer were right beside me in the "utility room." My mom only used the clothesline to air dry our bed sheets because she—and I—liked the fresh air smell they got. Even if I didn't wash my pants in the washer—they weren't all that dirty—I could tumble dry them for a while. I smiled, thinking how warm and cozy it would be to slip on a pair of jeans straight out of the dryer. I also knew how much my father complained about the electric bill, though, so I didn't even ask about running them through the dryer.

Feeling vulnerable and shivering from the rain trickling down my face and chest, I shucked off my jeans and spread them so the wet pants legs were inside the washing machine. My legs were still tanned from a summer spent running around in shorts and a bathing suit. I looked down at the two skinny, brown rails that ended at my pale white feet. They were pale because, except for when I was swimming at Steel Derrick, I always wore sneakers in the summer.

"Get upstairs and put some dry clothes on," my father said.

Without another word, I darted through the kitchen and dining room and went upstairs. I took the steps two at a time. When I entered the bedroom, Bobby was still asleep. Boy, was I glad.

I shucked off my damp t-shirt and rolled my undies down my legs. Shivering hard, my teeth chattering, I grabbed a clean shirt and underwear from my bureau and quickly put them on. Then, because I didn't want to break in a new pair of clean jeans, I pulled on my pajama bottoms. I wasn't going anywhere today, so I might as well get comfortable. At least once I was dressed, I didn't have to worry so much about my brother teasing me.

Leaving Bobby asleep, since the sky was lightening, I went back downstairs. I was already beginning to wonder what I was going to do with myself all day. We obviously weren't going anywhere. I just hoped my mom wouldn't try to get us to do something together as a family, like maybe read out loud together or play a board game. Those things—nice as they were—always ended badly, usually with me and my brother squabbling.

FIVE

It didn't take long for me to get bored.

Throughout the morning, the storm steadily picked up strength and intensity until it seemed as though what I had been out in earlier was nothing but a gusty day. I spent a lot of time moving from window to window, upstairs and down, looking out at the storm and the damage it was inflicting. To be honest, at least from the safety of the house, it wasn't so scary. Sure, leaves were blowing like crazy up the street and across the lawn in wild, swirling gusts, and some small branches had snapped off trees and now littered the lawn, but nothing looked as bad as I had imagined it. It was actually kind of fun. So far we had been lucky. Nothing had crashed through the roof or a window, and our electric power and phone were still working. Around noon, though, just as my mom was getting lunch ready, the lights flickered a few times. An instant later, they went out.

"God*damn* it!" my father roared.

He was down in the cellar, looking for any leaks

in the foundation. So far, he hadn't found any, but he was picking up what he could from the floor—boxes and crates and tools—and putting them on the array of work benches and tables he had down there to keep things dry. If there was a bad enough leak, I wondered what would happen to the freezer full of frozen food we kept down there. I moved over to the cellar door and looked down. All I could see was a wide pool of darkness as black as night at the foot of the stairs. After a few seconds of my dad stumbling around, muttering more curses and bumping into things, a flashlight beam came on, spearing the darkness like the welcomed beacon of a lighthouse. He must have found the one he kept on his workbench, although he was always yelling at me for playing with it and not putting it back where it belonged.

"Are you okay, dear?" my mom called out.

We had a gas stove, so she could continue frying bologna for our sandwiches. I don't know why, but she always made fried bologna sandwiches on white bread on storm days. Usually, that meant during a blizzard, but I guess—for whatever reason—my mother included hurricanes with blizzards.

"I'm fine, God*damn*it!" he shouted back.

"Language, Alan! Please!" she said.

From down in the basement, I heard some more sputtering curse words, but my dad spoke softly enough so I couldn't make out what he said. It wasn't like I hadn't heard or used them myself, but only with my friends. I'd have been skinned alive if my parents ever heard me swear.

"How long do you think the power will be out?" I asked my mom. Not having electricity made me more nervous than I wanted to admit.

With her back still to me, my mother said, "However long it takes them to get it back on."

That wasn't very helpful, but with the electricity out, that meant no TV, and *that* meant my brother— who had been sprawled on the couch in the living room all morning, watching TV—would get bored. And *that* usually meant he'd end up tormenting me, so I left the kitchen and, moving quickly through the living room, skedaddled upstairs to the bedroom.

I was panting lightly as I flopped down onto my bed. I figured there might be enough daylight coming through the window so I could read without needing a flashlight or candle. I was almost finished with *Tarzan and the Ant Men,* one of the best books in the series so far, and I wanted to finish it without interruption.

Of course, as soon as I hit my bed, I propped myself up with folded arms on the windowsill and looked out at the Big Tree. If I had been amazed by the punishment the Big Tree was taking this morning, now it was beyond belief. I sat there spellbound, watching.

The branches were bending and thrashing and blowing around so wildly they swept the ground and shredded the clouds overhead. It was like the whole tree was inside a gigantic blender, like the one at the soda fountain downtown in Tuck's Pharmacy. A puddle that seemed to widen even as I watched covered the ground underneath the Big Tree. The water was the color of strong tea. Its surface was as rippled as a washboard from the wind as water filled the area we had worn down playing and running around under the tree. It looked like it might already be ankle-deep. Wet leaves plastered like leeches to my window, obscuring my view, but I didn't dare open it to clean it off. I imagined the powerful wind sucking me right through the opening and up into the sky.

I lost track of the time as I stared at the Big Tree. My mind raced with scattered thoughts. I thought I might call Jimmy or Ray and see how they were doing, but I figured the phones had probably gone out when the electricity did. It would be insane to go out into the storm, anyway, and I knew my parents would say no, so I didn't even ask if I could go over to Jimmy's or if he could come over here. Besides, Jimmy was probably still mad at me for punching him so hard yesterday, even if I asked him over and he could come, he probably wouldn't. I satisfied myself, thinking he'd get over it. We got mad at each other all the time and quickly forgot about it.

Still, I was bored. As exciting as the *Tarzan* book was, it didn't draw me like it usually did. My dad had said he didn't want me or Bobby using the transistor radio because it would drain the batteries, which we might need if there was an emergency. I *certainly* wasn't going to do any *homework*. So what did that leave me?

It left me half-lying on my bed and staring out the window, watching the Big Tree and maybe… just maybe hoping to see the person—if it really was a person—I had seen or *thought* I had seen that morning. The crazy whirl of leaves and branches created a blur that made it impossible to see if anyone was really out there.

"Lunch!" my mother called from the foot of the stairs.

I was getting ready to get off the bed when to my

stunned amazement I saw one of the biggest branches on the Big Tree, one of the branches above the tree house, split from the main trunk and start to fall slowly. Even above the rushing hiss of wind and rain pelting my window, I could hear a long, slow crackling sound like a string of firecrackers going off. I stopped breathing in the time it took me to realize I was hearing the sound of splintering wood.

"*No!*" I said, but my throat was so tight the word was nothing more than a pathetic squeak. My breath sat like a lump of cold oatmeal in the center of my chest.

Leaning as close as I could to the window, I watched in utter disbelief, my body tingling with shock and horror—yes, *horror* as the huge branch slowly peeled itself away from the tree. The split widened slowly, and sharp, white splinters of newly exposed heartwood expanded like the hungry jaws of a shark, opening wide for its prey.

I stared, not blinking as the huge branch—as if it was in slow motion—crashed down, stripping leaves and branches away beneath its crushing weight. It came down on top of the tree house, flattening it in an instant. I could hear the boards we had sawed and nailed together snap like Popsicle sticks as the branch crushed them as easily as a foot coming down on an egg shell.

The falling branch hesitated for a terrible moment. Time froze like an insect in amber as I waited… waited for the branch to rise back up.

But that's not what happened.

Another powerful gust blasted into the tree, tearing through its limbs, and the branch and tree house came crashing down to the ground in a huge jumbled mess. Leaves were whisked away by the wind like black ashes from a bonfire.

By this time my heart was thumping with heavy hammer blows in the center of my chest. My throat was so dry I felt like I had inhaled flame. I couldn't believe what I was seeing. Frantic, I wanted to run downstairs and out the door or else climb out my window onto the roof and jump down to the ground so I could get to the wounded Big Tree as fast as I could before it died.

But I knew I was too late.

It was already gone.

I had the peculiar thought that, now that the damage was done, now that the Big Tree—or at least a large part of it—was down on the ground, the hurricane would stop. That, of course, is not what happened. The wind kept lashing the branches that lay on the ground, tearing like a huge scythe through the leaves on the branches that remained. The rain drove down hard, no longer in gusting sheets, but as a single dense curtain of dense gray, a shade or two lighter than the storm clouds tearing by overhead.

"Did you hear me?" my mother called from the foot of the stairs.

"Be right there," I answered, my voice sounded like a bullfrog's croak.

I realized I had been crying. My tears were warm and slick on my face. When I rubbed them away with the flat of my hand, it felt like my skin was oiled. A faint reflection of my face hovered in the window glass. A pit of grief opened up in my chest as I stared into my own eyes, but I wasn't exactly sure what it was I was grieving. Was it the destruction of the tree house or Big Tree itself?

I felt like I was trapped in the middle of a nightmare, but I snapped to quickly when I heard the rapid jackhammer sound of my brother, running up the stairs. I quickly wiped my face on the back of my forearm but was sure he would know I'd been crying if he saw my face. I settled myself on the bed, staring resolutely out the window so I wouldn't have to look at him.

The skin on the back of my neck tightened when Bobby entered the room, pushing the door open with such force it slammed against the bureau behind it, smashing up against the wall.

At least it's his bureau he's banging up, I thought every time he did it.

"What'cha doing?" he asked.

I chose not to answer him. Thank God he dropped onto his bed, sitting with his feet on the floor. I stared at his thin reflection in the window glass. In the dim lighting, he, too, looked like a ghost.

"I asked what you're doing?" he said.

There was a flurry of motion behind me, and then his pillow bounced off my shoulders and landed beside me on my bed.

"Nothing," I replied, hoping he didn't hear the knife edge of agony in my voice. It was difficult, fighting back my tears. They burned like pools of hot oil behind my eyes.

"Well Mom says lunch is ready, so come on down."

With that, he heaved himself off the bed and ran back downstairs.

Once Bobby was downstairs, I was left alone to silence broken only by the hammering sounds the fists of wind made when they hit the house and the steady splatter of rain against the windows. Beneath that was a low, steady roaring. As the wind flattened the tops of every tree I could see, I couldn't begin to imagine how many others along with telephone poles and other stuff had been knocked down.

"Your lunch is getting cold," my mother called, getting angry.

The aroma of fried bologna filled the stairwell as I started slowly down the stairs. I used the hem of my t-shirt to wipe my eyes, but I was positive they were rimmed with red and someone was going to ask me what the matter was.

Make no mistake; I wanted to cry. The sadness and grief that filled me was like no other I had experienced before. I remembered back when my grandmother—my mother's mother—had died in our house. She had been bedridden for more than two years before—mercifully—she died one night. Sometimes late at night, though, I can still hear her calling out from her bed in the guestroom down the hall from my bedroom. I'd always wanted that for my own bedroom so I wouldn't have to share one with Bobby, but my mother insisted that we had to have a guest bedroom for when relatives from Michigan or Florida visited. That's why I had to share a bedroom with my stupid brother. Sometimes late at night, though, I was grateful that I didn't sleep in that room because I was sure my grandmother's ghost still lingered there.

But I had been a little kid when "Mu-mu" was slowly dying—"dying by inches," my father had called it—but at the time, I didn't... I *couldn't* feel the depth of grief I felt now. Something really important in my life was dying... was already gone. I think for the first time in my life, I began to understand the meaning of loss because gone is gone forever.

"Is something the matter?" my mother asked after we sat down to eat. Fried bologna sandwiches had never been my favorite, but today the smell made my stomach churn. As I looked at her in the flickering glow of candles she had lit and set in the middle of the table, I forced a weak smile and said, "I'm aw'right."

It must have been my tone of voice that caught my brother's attention because he snapped his head up and looked at me with an expression I thought must be the last thing a mouse sees before the cat pounces.

"You've been crying," he said.

"Have not," I said even as a sour wave of grief filled my belly.

"Yes you have."

We sat next to each other. You'd think, with all the squabbling we did, my folks would make us sit on opposite sides of the table, but we didn't. Bobby turned in his seat and, half-facing me, gave my arm a hard little jab on the biceps.

"That's enough," my father said in his *I mean business* voice.

"What a little baby," my brother said, not willing to let it go just yet. I knew he'd push until one of my parents—usually my dad—exploded, and then we'd both get blamed.

"Shaddup," I said so softly I didn't think he could hear me.

"What are you afraid of? You think the hurricane's gonna blow the house down or something."

"I said shaddup!"

"What a little baby."

My father slapped the table with his open palm.

"I said *enough!*" and this time his tone of voice was sharp enough to make Bobby turn quickly back to his meal. I stared at mine on the plate, unable to imagine how I was going to swallow a single bite.

"Are you all right?" my mother asked, leaning close to me. She placed her hand on my forehead and held it there a few seconds, and said, "You're not feverish."

"I'm fine," I said, cringing inwardly at the whining tone in my voice. "I just don't feel like eating is all."

"Well eat up anyway," my dad said as he pushed the last bit of sandwich into his mouth. His jaw muscles snapped back and forth as he chewed. Then he took a huge gulp of milk to wash it all down.

"So what are we gonna do?" I asked, hoping to change the subject.

"We'll just have to wait it out," my mom said.

I wanted the storm to be over so I could go outside. I was desperate to get to the Big Tree and see exactly how much damage the storm had done. In my mind, the devastation was complete. I hoped I was exaggerating, but I had seen that falling branch pulverize our tree house. I was so crazy to get outside and check out the wreckage that it felt like lines of ants were crawling up my sides to my armpits.

Somehow I managed to gag down half my sandwich, and when it was obvious I wasn't going to finish, my father reached over and took the other half, saying, "No need for it to go to waste."

"It'll go to your waist," my mom said, but she had said that so often my dad acted as if she hadn't even spoken as he took a large bite and chewed. My dad liked to eat and had the belly to prove it.

After lunch, the rest of the family pretty much minded their own business. Bobby took his usual place on the couch in the living room and actually settled down to read a book. For Bobby to read *anything* without being told to was an absolute miracle. That was more than enough proof that he, too, was profoundly bored.

My dad went back down into the cellar to check for leaks. He asked me to come along, but I told him I was fine... I had some homework to do. While my mom busied herself in the kitchen, I went back upstairs. Sitting on my bed and staring out at the fallen tree—at least the huge portion that had fallen—I felt like crying again.

But I also was angry... and worried.

I was angry because this had happened, and I still couldn't believe the testimony of my own eyes. As I looked at the skyline above the Big Tree, I could see a huge opening where the branch used to be. Now there was a hole, like a gap-toothed grin, in the piece of the world I used to be able to see from my bed. Soot-gray clouds scudding by on the wind, being torn to tatters as they raced out to sea.

I was worried because I was already keenly aware of what I had lost. It wasn't just the copies of *Playboy* and other secrets we had stashed up there. It wasn't that we'd have to rebuild the tree house. We could do that. It was that somehow—even then—I already knew that we wouldn't rebuild it, and that losing it and the Big Tree was going to mark my life.

I had no idea how much.

SIX

Evening came on so subtly that I barely noticed the gradual darkening. The clouds loomed low, filling the sky as if there was a gigantic oil fire somewhere in the neighborhood. But I knew from what I heard coming over my dad's battery powered transistor radio that this storm covered a huge portion of New England and New York State.

At some point, Bobby came upstairs and knocked around for a while before going into the bathroom. Lately, I'd noticed that he spent quite a bit of time in the bathroom with the door locked. My mother noticed this, too, and I caught her a few times giving a funny look at my dad, as though she wanted or expected him to say something to Bobby about why he was taking so long in there. I knew what he was up to. I'd been getting boners since it seemed like forever, but I never played with my wiener like Bobby did.

"You gonna just sit on your bed all day?" Bobby asked when he finally came out of the bathroom. His

47

cheeks were flushed, and I noticed that his right hand was trembling slightly. He had a shifty look, too, like he was feeling guilty about something.

I kept my back to him, trying my best to ignore him, but that usually irritated him even more than anything I said or did. I shrank away from him as he approached my bed. The floorboards creaked beneath his weight. My shoulders bunched up until the muscles began to thrum like guitar strings. I cringed, waiting for the hammer to fall as I carefully watched his dim reflection in the window panes.

I rolled over to one side and, with a snap of my body like I was doing a tumbling move in gym class, leaped to my feet. Before Bobby could react, I was halfway to the bedroom door when my mom called up to us that it was time for supper.

Already? I thought? The half of fried bologna sandwich was still sitting like a cold lump in the pit of my stomach. But I went down the stairs, taking them two at a time because I was sure Bobby was right behind me, ready to jab me in the back if he got close enough.

Supper was like lunch. I still didn't have an appetite. What little conversation there was centered around the hurricane. My dad had been listening to the transistor radio off and on all day. He wanted to conserve the battery in case the power was off for more than a day or two. Usually when we lost power during a storm, the electricity came back within a few hours, and that was during a blizzard. I tried to imagine what it was like for the electric company workers to be out in the weather… or maybe they were staying home, too, until the storm was over, and the cleanup began.

"You've done nothing but mope up in your room all day. Are you sure you're feeling all right?" my mother asked, and then—true to form—she reached across the table and pressed the flat of her hand against my forehead, feeling for a temperature.

I hadn't liked this kind of attention for a long time, now, and I pulled away from her, scowling.

"I'm not sick!" I said. "I never said I was."

Bobby cast a wary look at me as if warning me that he'd pop me a good one if I didn't stop whining.

Although I wasn't hungry, I finished my supper. It was one of my favorites—steak, mashed potato, and green beans—but I can't say as I enjoyed it. In fact, the food struck me as flavorless, and I started to wonder if maybe something was wrong with me. What if something had changed inside me?

After supper, my mother suggested we bring the candles and oil lamps into the living room and play *Monopoly* or *Scrabble*, but I told her that maybe I *was* feeling a bit out of sorts and that I maybe should go straight to bed. She and my dad both gave me quizzical looks as if they suspected I was trying to set up an excuse to miss school tomorrow, but I was pretty sure there wouldn't be school anyway… not with the electricity still off.

Leaving the candles and oil lamps behind and carrying a small flashlight, I followed the bouncing, wavering splotch of light up the stairs.

I changed into my pajamas and climbed into bed. I lay there for I don't know how long listening to the sudden hard gusts of wind hammer the sides of the house. The rafters creaked, and the hissing spray of rain against the windows sounded like someone had upset a nest of snakes.

Sometime later, Bobby came upstairs, but I was already half asleep and barely noticed it when he got into bed. At some point in the night, though, my eyes suddenly snapped open. I was wide awake.

Something was wrong.

I don't know how I knew it or why it had awakened me, but I sat up and looked all around, trying to see what the problem was. The room seemed to be much darker than it should have been. Functioning on automatic, I reached out and fumbled around for the lamp at the head of my bed. When I finally found it and snapped it on, nothing happened. There was no harsh glare of light like I'd been expecting.

Of course not.

The hurricane had taken down the wires.

But as I sat there in the darkness, breathing lightly through my teeth, I finally realized what was wrong.

The wind and rain had stopped.

Is it over? I wondered as a thrill raced through me.

The hush that filled my bedroom… and the world… was astounding. I had gotten so used to hearing the rain lash the house and the deep, vibrating howl of the wind that I missed it now. Other than my racing heart, the only other sounds were the deep, steady breathing of my sleeping brother and the far off dripping of running water.

I wanted to wake up Bobby and ask if he had any idea what was going on, but the expression "Let sleeping dogs lie" echoed in my head.

Instead, moving as quietly as possible, I unfastened the lock on the window beside my bed and, placing the heels of both palms on the wider edge, pushed up. The window scraped loudly in its old wooden frame, and the lead counterweights inside the wall made a dull drumming sound. I cringed, but the sound wasn't enough to wake my brother.

I sighed as I brought my face close to the window screen and inhaled. The night air carried an intoxicating mixture of fresh, wet dirt smell and the damp aroma of crushed leaves and tree sap. I looked at the trees on the horizon. They resembled black lace against the soot gray sky, but not a branch... not a leaf stirred in the eerie stillness.

For a moment, I thought I must be dreaming. Then I remembered my dad telling me about the "eye" of the hurricane—the center of the storm—there's a calm spot that the winds all twist around.

We must be in the eye... and if we are, that means the storm's only half over.

A cold pit opened up in my stomach, and I wondered if our house would last through the second half of the storm.

Outside, the night was a solid wall of darkness except for a tiny hint of light—a faint, flickering yellow glow that shone in Old Lady Wayrenen's living room window next door. I wondered if she was awake and, finding herself alone, was fretting, like I was, about the storm and the weird silence. Maybe one of her sons, realizing she might be confused and frightened, had come over to her house in the momentary calm and was sitting up with her. I couldn't see the candle directly. Its diffused glow barely illuminated the window frame.

I stared at the illusive glow to make sure it was there. My eyes shifted back and forth as the light wavered and dimmed in the darkness. I wondered if the light was really there or if it was the glow of the moon on the front of her house, shining through a break in the clouds. Looking up at the sky, though, I saw that there was no way the moon could be shining through that thick blanket of clouds.

If the light isn't coming from Old Lady Wayrenen's house, where's it coming from?

That's when my gaze shifted over to the Big Tree.

In the darkness of the night, I could see a huge, black shape on the ground. It looked like a large elephant or maybe a dinosaur had collapsed and died on Old Lady Wayrenen's front lawn, but I knew what it was. In the darkness, however, my imagination created all sorts of impossible things.

I turned my head, pressing my ear against the screen, and listened. The hushed stillness outside created a weird vacuum inside my head. It took me a long time to realize that something else was weird.

There was no sound. No crickets… No birds… No sign of any life.

I wondered if every living creature was hiding or if the storm had killed or swept them all away.

My mind was racing, and all the while, I stared at the Big Tree. I saw things… or I *imagined* I saw things… shifting about in the darkness. Branches and leaves shifted even though there wasn't the faintest breath of wind. I strained to listen, but the only sound was the ruffling thump of my pulse in my ears.

I realized I couldn't depend on my eyesight. It kept jiggling and shifting, and I found it all but impossible to focus directly on anything for long before it shifted and melted away. I began to realize— I became *convinced* I could see… something… a vague, indistinct shape moving about on the ground around the fallen branch of the Big Tree.

"What the…?" I murmured, loud enough to disturb Bobby. He rolled over in his bed and muttered in a sleep-thick voice, "Shaddup, will yah?"

I waited, poised and tense to hear if he was going to get out of bed. Maybe he woke up and had to pee… or maybe he was going to go into the bathroom for some other reason. The last thing I wanted was to get punched from behind in the darkness. My shoulders hunched as I waited for the blow to fall, but after a moment or two, Bobby started breathing heavily again, and I knew he'd fall back to sleep.

Once I knew I was safe—at least for the time being—I turned my attention back to the Big Tree. It was frustrating to stare into the black void below my bedroom window. I felt disoriented, like I was looking down into an abandoned well. I'm not sure when it happened, but at some point I realized a faint glow was hovering like a flickering candle in the downed foliage. It looked like the full moon barely discernible through a thick blanket of clouds.

"What the heck?" I whispered, so surprised I didn't even worry about disturbing my brother.

I wondered if, somehow, this had something to do with the candle shining in Old Lady Wayrenen's window. Maybe it was reflecting off the damp leaves or something. But the light I was looking at had an odd blue radiance, and the longer I stared at it, the more I became convinced that it was a face.

Impossible!

An icy thrill ran up my spine.

I stared harder, and the face became more defined, glowing with a pale ivory light. I thought I could make out two dark pits where the eyes should be and another dark smudge where the mouth was,

RICK HAUTALA

but I wasn't sure.

I was frozen with fear.

I'm sure I let out a faint whimper when I realized that whoever or whatever was out there was looking up at me.

The face—if that's what it was—had soft, rounded features… like a girl with dark hair hanging down on both sides of her face. Her eyes were wide, and she stared at me without blinking. My heart stopped beating. My breath caught in my chest like a knot of barbed wire. I felt exposed… naked. I wanted to duck down out of sight below the windowsill and stay out of sight, but it was already too late.

She or whoever had already seen me, and I was paralyzed with fear. Every muscle, every nerve in my body was locked. I remembered that Greek myth about the monster Medusa, and I had the panicky thought that maybe that's who was out there.

Medusa.

And I had looked into her eyes and was already turning into stone.

It took immense effort, but somehow I clenched my hand into a fist and squeezed it tightly to convince myself that I wasn't really turning into stone. All the while, I kept staring down at the faint glowing sphere, more convinced than ever that someone really was down there… and looking at me in the upstairs window.

"Hi," I whispered, raising a hand in greeting.

My voice was no more than a breathy whisper, but was that an answering greeting from the figure below, or had the wind begun to pick up again?

"Hello."

My breath could hardly carry the distance to the

Big Tree, but I was determined to find out if someone was out there and, if there was, *who* it was.

SEVEN

As I crept downstairs, it seemed like every stair creaked underfoot. I had dressed in silence and was wearing the t-shirt and jeans I'd worn the day before. My sneakers were in the utility room by the back door where I had left them after going outside early in the morning. I could hardly believe it had been just this morning. It seemed like ages ago.

I had my flashlight stuffed into my back pocket, but I didn't turn it on yet. Rounding the corner at the bottom of the stairs, I had to feel my way around by running my hands along the wall and furniture in the dining room. I was afraid I might bump into something and wake up my parents, but I made it into the kitchen without incident. I wondered if my folks were already awake. The lull in the storm might have broken into their sleep, too. I had to be perfectly quiet, but I was practiced at this. I pretended I was an Apache, sneaking up on a sleeping settler's family. I couldn't count the number of nights I had crept downstairs like this, either for a midnight snack or to sneak outside and meet up with my friends who had also snuck out.

For some reason, though, tonight seemed more serious.

I maybe didn't know it consciously, but I certainly sensed that something really big was happening. It wasn't just the hurricane. Even as I wedged my bare feet into my sneakers, I was filled with the conviction that something or someone was waiting for me outside… something that was going to change my life.

My palms were slick with sweat as I slowly turned the doorknob to the backdoor. When the bolt clicked, it sounded as loud as gunfire going off inside the house. I tensed, waiting to see if my parents had heard it and if my father had gotten up to check out what had made that sound, but the house was filled with dense, sleeping silence.

Slowly, I turned the doorknob and pulled the door open. I was prepared for the hurricane winds to suddenly start blowing hard again and rip the screen door from my hand, but the door opened slowly, and then I pushed the screen door open. I heaved a sigh of relief when I stepped out onto the back porch and eased the door shut behind me.

Outside, the air seemed as thick as honey, impossible to breathe. The porch was covered with leaves and twigs that had blown down from nearby trees. The leaves were slick underfoot, like the porch had been greased. Like I usually did, instead of using the steps, I jumped off the side of the porch and hit the ground. It was saturated with rain water, and I landed with a splash that instantly soaked my jeans up to my knees. I lost my balance and almost fell but, thankfully, didn't.

Panting heavily, I looked around as if I expected to see someone—probably my brother—had seen my lack of coordination and was going to give me a hard time about it, but the sense of being utterly alone in the dark was unnerving. I looked across the yard and driveway toward the Big Tree and was amazed—once again—to see how much of the tree *wasn't* where it should be. It was lying in a heap on the ground and looked two-dimensional in the darkness.

I started slowly across the yard. I didn't plan to turn on my flashlight until after I checked for the candle in Old Lady Wayrenen's house. Her window was dark. The feeling that I was being watched hadn't gone away, and I wondered if she might be sitting there in the darkness, looking outside... watching me. If anything, the feeling got more intense, but I was also sure *if* someone was watching me, they were lurking in the downed branches.

What if it's not a person?

A cold wave of goose bumps washed across my arms in spite of the warm, damp night air.

What if it's a wolf or a bear?

I knew there hadn't been any bears or wolves in our area in a long time, but that didn't stop my overactive imagination.

Or maybe it's something worse... like a vampire or a ghost?

Stop it!

I crossed the driveway and started down the slight slope to the boundary between our yard and Old Lady Wayrenen's. There was no fence to mark the property line, although a low hedge of forsythia ran about half the length. But there was nothing between me and the Big Tree, so once I was as safe from being spotted as I was ever going to be, I grabbed my flashlight and clicked it, directing it at the Big Tree.

I was stunned by what I saw.

Sitting on the thickest part of the downed branch was a girl. She was wearing a thin, white thing that looked like a nightgown. Rain had plastered it against her body, and beneath damp ripples, I could clearly see the outline of her body. She raised her arms to shield her eyes from the light.

I couldn't believe it.

I stood there in silence, the night pressing in all around me. My mouth was hanging open like I was a fish going for the hook. Her arms and what I could see of her face were as pale as weathered marble, like she was a statue, come to life. She was sitting on the fallen branch with her bare feet dangling in the air maybe three or four feet off the ground. When she looked at me from under the protection of her hand, her eyes were deep and dark. They glistened as though made of shiny balls of tar.

"Are you… are you real?" I asked. In the darkness, my voice sounded weak and muffled.

The girl—if that's what she was—said nothing. She was still shading her eyes, and I finally realized I should shine the beam of light away from her face. As soon as I shifted it to one side so it illuminated a spot of foliage, she lowered her hand. In the dense gloom, I could still see her features. They were soft and round, but they seemed to fade into the black night. She was definitely a little girl, but she sure as heck wasn't anyone I knew from the neighborhood.

"So?" I said. "Are you…?"

"Real?" she said, finishing the question for me.

Her voice had a faint, rising lilt that did something strange to me. It both chilled and warmed me at the same time. It brushed against my eardrums with a vaguely familiar sound… like leaves, fluttering in a gentle breeze or the faint flapping of a butterfly's wings. At the same time, there was a depth and resonance, like a pulse or a distant drumbeat.

"Yeah," I said. "Real…"

I wanted to move closer to her so I could determine if she was even there. I wondered if I might be dreaming, or if this was some kind of hallucination, but I didn't dare take a step closer. Something was warning me that this girl—if she really was a girl and if she really was there—was dangerous in spite of her apparent frailty.

Craning her head back and rolling it slowly from side to side, she looked all around as if trying to take in the scope of the Big Tree and the damage it had suffered. Her eyes glistened in the dark with a weird quicksilver light. After a long moment, she stopped looking around and turned to gaze directly at me. She extended one hand as though for me to grasp it, but then she flexed her fingers and waved them in front of her face.

"I *am* real," she said with a distant, dreamy voice. It sounded like she was trying to convince herself as much as me. "At least I think I am."

She looked harmless enough, but I still wasn't sure.

Maybe she had been visiting friends or family in the neighborhood, and maybe she—like me—had gotten up and come outside into the calm as the hurricane's eye passed over.

Maybe she was some neighbor's idiot cousin or

someone who was mentally not all there and had wandered away from the house she was staying in, and now she was lost and confused and scared. Maybe a falling branch had clunked her on the head, and she had amnesia or something.

"Can you help me?" she asked.

The sad, pleading note in her voice drew me closer against my will. I took two quick steps toward her.

"I... I'm not sure," I replied. "What's the matter?"

My question seemed to confuse her. She cocked her head to one side and, when she frowned, thin, dark lines wrinkled her forehead like a washboard. The lines around her eyes made her look suddenly as old as Old Lady Wayrenen. I caught my breath and held it, waiting for her to say something more, but the silence that enveloped the world went on uninterrupted.

As she looked around again, taking in the Big Tree and the fallen branch, tears gathered in her eyes in shimmering pools. They glowed so brightly in the dark I was suddenly convinced I had to be imagining this... all of it... her and the Big Tree and everything. I told myself I had to be in bed, asleep and dreaming.

"I... I've lost my home," she said in a shattered voice. Her lower lip shivered even though the night air didn't feel all that cold to me. Then again, I wasn't wearing a thin, wet nightgown. I figured she must have been in bed and had run out of the house into the storm in a panic.

"So, where—uh, where do you live?"

I was positive she wasn't from my neighborhood. I knew everyone on my street and most of the streets connected to it. So unless she was visiting someone who lived nearby that I hadn't heard about, she was a long way from any "home" she said she had lost.

Her eyes, as big and bright as silver dollars hovered in the darkness, wide with fright when a sudden gust of wind came up and rustled the leaves around us. They clattered like skeleton hands, applauding. I looked up at the sky through the foliage and saw hints of dark clouds shifting against darker clouds. I knew what was happing. The eye of the hurricane was passing, and the storm was coming back. I remembered hearing my father say something about how the second half of the hurricane is usually stronger than the first. I was going to have to get back inside soon if I didn't want to die, but at that moment, I wasn't all that concerned for myself.

I was worried about this girl, whoever she was.

"What's your name?" I asked, trying to keep the edge out of my voice.

I jumped when, suddenly, a thin piping sound filled the night. Again, I looked around nervously. The feeling in the air was like a heavy weight suspended above my head about to come crashing down before I could see it.

"Sylvia," she finally said, her voice as low and soft as the gathering wind. I could hear tension bordering on stark terror in her voice, and it made me worry all the more.

"So where do you live?"

The wind was picking up rapidly, blowing in fitful gusts that hissed over the saturated grass and shook the leaves. Overhead, the branches of the Big Tree—those that were left, anyway, clattered like old bones.

Sylvia turned her head, looking left and right.

Tears were streaming down her cheeks now like shimmering rivers of mercury. I had the clear sensation that she could see things I couldn't. The thought that something was approaching—fast—worked on my nerves like a rat, gnawing on a gunny sack. Sylvia's cheeks gleamed unnaturally bright in the darkness. I was still half-convinced there was no way she could be real. She must be a ghost or something. I wanted to ask her to prove to me that she was real, but how could she do that? Icy fear had a grip on my throat like an unseen hand, choking me.

"I have to go," she said, her voice so thin it seemed to whip away on the rising wind.

"Where?" I asked. "Where can you go? Who are you staying with? You're not even from around here, are you?"

My sudden flurry of questions seemed to frighten her, and she looked at me as if she didn't understand anything I was saying. I was afraid for myself, but I was more afraid for her. There was no way she could stay out here... not on a night like this. She might get hurt or even die.

"So tell me where you live."

I had to shout, now, because the wind had suddenly kicked up, and a fine drifting mist of rain was beginning to fall. It was going to get bad really fast, and I hated to think that she would be out here alone with no place to go.

"Come with me," I said as I held my hand out to her. I shivered, suddenly sure that when—*if*—she touched me, her hand would prove insubstantial and pass through mine.

Sylvia looked up at me with the most forlorn expression I had ever seen. I flashed on a memory of the look my cat, Hasty, had given me when my father had accidentally run her over in the driveway, crushing her lower spine. Unable to walk, she had collapsed there on the driveway, looking up at me as if to ask me what had happened and why I wasn't doing anything about it. Her eyes were glazed with pain. My heart gave a deep, heavy thud, and I knew that not all the moisture on my face was from the rain.

"You have to come with me. You can stay in my house," I said

Sylvia kept staring at me, her face a pale oval that seemed to fade back into the dark gloom of the fallen branches. I had the weird impression that she was receding from me like someone slowly... silently drifting away from the shore in a boat.

I kept holding my hand out to her. At first, she didn't raise hers to touch mine. She continued to stare at me with the saddest, most longing expression I'd ever seen. Then, ever so slowly, with the wind whipping around me now, she raised her hand.

When we touched, I knew instantly that it wasn't just in my imagination when a jolt of electricity passed up my wrist and wrapped around my arm. The tingling sensation was frightening and incredibly exciting, and filled me with a strange warmth, almost fever-like. I felt a sense of longing for something, something I had no words for. I have no idea what kind of expression was on my face. I might have looked shocked; I might have been smiling like an idiot; I just as easily could have been wincing in pain. My breath was raw in my throat, and my eyes were wide and staring down at her luminous face.

I don't know how long our hands were touching,

but I shook myself back to awareness when a sudden downpour drenched me to the bone. Water whisked over me as a hammer-fisted gust of wind slammed against my back, almost knocking me over. Leaves suddenly tore from the Big Tree in a huge gust and slapped my face and arms with nettle-like stings.

"Please," I said. I was filled with a sudden desperate fear that she would be blown away. Her grip on my hand was loosening, and even as I watched, her face started pulling back, dissolving… disappearing into the darkness under the Big Tree. Her face kept receding until it was like I was looking at her through the wrong end of a telescope.

"You can't stay out here!" I had to shout to be heard above the rising storm. "You'll die if you stay out here."

A faint smile twitched the corners of her mouth, but there was no humor—only grim acceptance as her face dimmed… and dimmed… until—finally—it was nothing more than a gray smudge on the night… and then it winked out.

She was gone.

EIGHT

Somehow—I have no idea how—I made it back to the house with the wind and rain punching and slashing at me. My sneakers, jeans, and shirt were as wet as if I had taken a dive into the ocean. The lawn was so saturated with rainwater I kept slipping and sliding as if I were walking on grease. With every other step, I stopped and, shielding my face with both hands, looked back to the tree, hoping to see Sylvia, but there was no sign of her. The roaring howl of the storm rose all around me, but as I stared into the darkness, I was sure I could hear her heart-rending sobs and her voice, calling to me... asking... begging for me to help her.

The screen door blew out of my hands and almost flew away when I opened it. I held onto it and opened the inside door with my other hand. I slipped into the house, and try as I might, I could not manage to close both doors behind me without letting go of the screen door. A blast of wind blew it shut behind me. It sounded like a cannon shot in the dark, and I held my breath, straining my eyes in the darkness, watching for the yellow shaft of a flashlight beam that would mean my father was awake and I was going to get it for real this time.

But nothing happened. They slept on.

I tiptoed up the stairs, uncharacteristically taking them one at a time. The house was creaking and thumping as the storm drove its full force against it. I went into the bathroom and shucked off my wet clothes, leaving them in a pile on the bathroom floor. Naked and shivering, I toweled myself off and then went back to the bedroom and slid on some clean, dry underwear.

I didn't lie down and go to sleep right away, though. Instead, I perched myself with my arms braced on the windowsill and stared out at the storm and the black, swaying mass of what was left of the Big Tree. I turned my flashlight on and tried shining the beam down at it, but the light reflected off the glass, making it impossible to see outside. Still, I thought it was a good way to signal to Sylvia that I hadn't forgotten about her even though I hadn't done a darned thing to help, I clicked the light off and on, and swung it back and forth several times, hoping she'd see my signal.

Finally, though, in spite of all the excitement, I got sleepy and lay down. I had trouble falling asleep with the wind and rain slamming against the house. That would have been enough to keep me up, but I was also worried about Sylvia, wondering where she was and what she was doing. It didn't matter to me if she was real or something I had imagined. Either way, thinking about her made it almost impossible to drift off. Throughout the rest of the night, my sleep was haunted by visions of her pale, luminous face, floating like a helium balloon in the darkness, and her voice—faint, desperate, pleading—asking me to help her.

NINE

Morning came with a bang… a stinging slap on the butt, that is, courtesy of my brother. I rolled over and kicked at him, but he was practiced in the art of bullying me, and he darted away from my kick, so I missed him by several inches.

"Dad says you gotta up," Bobby said.

"How come?" I asked.

Before he answered, I shifted around, moaning as I dropped both feet to the floor. Leaning forward, I rubbed my face with both hands like I had splashed it with cold water, but then, like a bolt of lightning, the memory of last night slammed into me like a freight train careening out of the fog.

Last night… The hurricane… The Big Tree… Sylvia.

Stifling a scream, I turned around quickly and looked out my window toward the Big Tree.

It was still raining, and the wind was still blowing hard, but not as much as before. Maybe the storm was finally petering out. Right away, I saw that at least one part of what I remembered from last night had been real.

Branches—some of them thicker than my waist—and leaves and roughly-sawed boards lay scattered on the grass beneath the Big Tree. Huge puddles of muddy water the color of melted chocolate dotted Old Lady Wayrenen's lawn, and the street was so covered with water it looked more like a river. Overhead, the clouds were thinning out as they scudded by, torn like old curtains blown out over the ocean.

When I sniffed, trying not to cry, Bobby—ever the predator for the tiniest trace of misery—caught on. Kneeling on the edge of my bed, he looked outside. It didn't take him long to figure out what was upsetting me.

"Holy crap," he said. "The Big Tree's destroyed."

"Most of it," I said. I didn't like hearing him confirm what I knew but wanted to deny, but he was right. The Big Tree was all but stripped of leaves, and the branches that had fallen off left less than half of the original tree still standing. It was a skeleton of its former self. A sudden fear gripped me that Jimmy's Uncle Walt would decide to cut the rest of it down to be rid of it.

"That sucks," my brother said, sounding genuinely upset even though he no longer hung out at the tree with us. He was always off with his own friends, John Halman and Roy Lee. Like me, my brother swore when he was with his friends but never when our parents might hear us. Even something as innocuous as "suck" might get us grounded for a couple of days or a week. Then we'd end up doing work, usually in the yard. My father called it "punishment duty." No wonder, even today, I look upon manual labor as a punitive exercise, rather than something one does for pleasure or profit.

When Bobby looked at me, I thought I could see something like genuine sympathy in his expression. Maybe, I thought, he wasn't such a jerk after all. It was strange for my brother to express even the slightest genuine emotion other than spite.

"So what're you gonna do?" he asked.

"What do you mean?"

"'Bout the tree house and what you've got stashed out there?"

I knew he meant the *Playboys*, but I didn't want to admit that I had them. I'd never told him about them, so unless one of my friends told him—which wasn't too likely—he must have been snooping around up there and found them.

"Mom and Dad find out about 'em, you'll get skinned."

I wondered why he had this sudden concern for me getting into trouble. The only thing I could think was he either wanted to take the magazines away from me or else he had his own secrets stashed somewhere and didn't want to risk getting found out.

"I know," I said, nodding while I mentally sifted through my options. The most obvious one was that I should get outside sooner rather than later so I could clean up and throw away any evidence.

"You think, like, if Walt or Jussi finds 'em they'll tell Mom and Dad?" I asked.

My brother shrugged as if he could just about care.

"Walt'd probably keep them for himself. You've seen them pictures he has on the walls in the horse barn, right?"

I nodded, remembering all too well the funny feelings I got when I had first seen them a couple of years ago. They were calendars, with women wearing underwear that looked nothing like the kind of underwear I saw on clotheslines in the neighborhood.

"You didn't have them wrapped up in, like, plastic or tin foil, did you?" he asked.

Biting my lower lip, I shook my head. It was sad to imagine that they had already turned into a mess of water-soaked pulp. Then again, the magazines were the least of my worries.

"Then don't sweat it," Bobby said. "They're probably ruined now, anyway."

I nodded again, but the truth was, I could just about give a crap about those magazines. I was still worried about Sylvia. I couldn't imagine she had survived the night without taking shelter somewhere.

But where?

"I can't wait 'till this fucking storm is over," I said. My voice was low and tight with intensity, but it carried far enough, apparently, for my mother to hear. At that moment, she was about halfway up the stairs to see what we were up to.

"What did you just say?" she said as she pushed the bedroom door all the way open and appeared, glowering, in the doorway. Her eyes were wide with shock, her lips thin and pale.

"Uh-oh," my brother said in an irritating sing-song voice as he backed away from me. He didn't want to catch any collateral damage.

I did what any boy my age would do.

I lied.

"Nothing," I said.

My mother glared at me, at a total loss for words.

Her hand gripping the doorknob started to shake so badly I had a fleeting mental image that she was about to rip the door off its hinges and fling it at me.

"You'd better *not*," was all she said. I was sure from the flush on her cheeks that she had heard me loud and clear, and that she would eventually tell my father what she heard *his* youngest son mutter.

We stared at each other for the longest time. My pulse was hammering with quick, muffled beats in my head, and I was afraid to speak because I was sure my voice would be so high-pitched my mother would know I was lying to her.

"Well, breakfast is about ready, so why don't you both come downstairs," she said. As she said this, she never broke eye contact with me. I withered under her unblinking gaze, wishing she would let this drop. After another lengthening moment of tense silence, though, she backed away from the doorway, then turned and went downstairs.

My brother looked at me, his face twisted up with glee.

"You are such an *idiot*," was all he said. Before I could say anything, he also left the room. I was left standing there, my stomach feeling as hollow as a Hallowe'en pumpkin as I looked out the window at the dense, gray sky that showed no sign of the hurricane ending.

~ * ~

"So," my mother said as the four of us sat down to breakfast.

She had overdone it with the meal, making what we usually only had on Sunday morning before going

75

to church or when we had family from out of state visiting. I was nervous, thinking she might have already mentioned to my father that I had used the F-word, but I couldn't tell by the way he looked or acted if she had or not. I felt like a criminal waiting for the blade of the guillotine to drop.

I ate fast, wanting to get away from the table as soon as I could, so I stuffed myself with scrambled eggs, bacon, toast, home fries, and orange juice. When I was done—in record time—I felt logy enough to go back to bed. With the hurricane still blowing, the power still out, and nothing much to do, I cleared my place, putting my plate, silverware, and juice glass into the sink, and went back upstairs. Sitting on my bed with my back against the wall, I tried to get into the *Tarzan* book, but there was no way I could focus on the story. I kept turning around and looking out my window at the damaged Big Tree.

And wondering about Sylvia.

I was feeling guilty for being safe and warm and full of food. We were lucky to have a gas stove so my mom could still make hot meals. I wondered if Sylvia had gone home… wherever that was… or if she was still out there, hiding in the downed branches of the Big Tree.

A sudden chill ran through me when I wondered if she had died during the night.

Every time I looked outside, I half-convinced myself I could see her face in the foliage. I knew my mind was playing tricks on me because the wind would suddenly gust, the leaves would blow aside, and I would see that she wasn't there after all. It was only an illusion created by the leaves and branches.

But there were a few times when I was *positive* I

could see her looking up at me and silently condemning me because I was warm, safe, and dry.

After a while, I got drowsy. I hadn't slept all that well last night, and there wasn't anything I had to do today, so I put my book aside and settled down on my bed, lying on my stomach with my eyes closed. The deep-throated roar of the wind and the hissing spray and splatter of rain against the window screen created a white noise that gently lulled me into sleep. Before long, I was dead to the world.

I don't know how long I was asleep. I remember at one point hearing Bobby come into the room and saying something to me, but I was too deep to respond.

The sound of the storm became a cacophony that rose and faded, blended and mixed with other sounds... sounds that seemed to come from inside my head.

I wasn't sure when I began to hear it, but at some vague, dreamy point, I was aware that someone was crying. It wasn't a full-out wailing cry. It was softer, gentler... like someone close beside me that I couldn't see was sobbing. The sound filled me with sadness so deep I couldn't begin to describe, much less understand it. Tears welled up in my eyes

Maybe I'm crying in my sleep? I thought, feeling curiously detached from my emotions.

I rolled onto my back and swiped a hand across my eyes.

Nope.

No tears.

I took a deep breath and heard it shudder in my chest the same way the wind was roaring outside, mere inches from where my head rested on my pillow.

Is Bobby doing something to me… trying to trick me?

I wouldn't have put it past him, but why would he or anyone else pretend to be crying… and it sounded so genuine.

I took another breath and groaned as I rolled my head from side to side, feeling the warm well of my pillow. At some point, I decided to open my eyes, but when I did, I was almost immediately aware of… something that was blocking my view of the sky. I let out a stifled cry and scrambled backwards, almost falling off my bed when I realized someone was outside my window, sitting on the utility room roof and looking in at me.

The sound of the wind was drowned out by the rapid whooshing sound that filled my head as my vision cleared, and I saw that it was Sylvia. Her face was inches from the window screen as she squatted on the peak of the roof, her legs splayed to both sides of her body so her knees almost reached her ears. She leaned forward, one hand resting on the windowsill. The other, she lifted to her lips and made a hushing motion. I focused on her hands and noticed that her fingernails were deep blue… almost purple. I thought it was from the damp cold. When I looked up into her eyes, I caught a shimmering green glow that fluttered like leaves in the wind.

I got to my knees slowly and rubbed my eyes, unable to believe what I was seeing. I was convinced I must still be asleep and dreaming this, but when I reached out my hand toward her, she responded by raising one hand in silent greeting. I pressed mine, palm out, on the window glass, and she did the same thing, putting her hand against the screen.

Moving slowly and keeping my hand in place, I shifted so I was kneeling on both knees and brought my face so close to the window my breath fogged the glass.

"Are you…? How did you…?"

I had no idea what I wanted to say, but when I realized I was speaking out loud and that someone downstairs might hear me, I stopped talking and simply looked at her in disbelief.

What was she doing out there?

How had she gotten up onto the roof, especially in the wind and rain?

What did she want?

An image from *Dracula*, which I had read last summer and not really liked, came to mind, and I was suddenly afraid that she was a vampire out to suck my blood.

But… no.

She couldn't be a vampire. If she was, she would have sucked my blood last night when she had me alone in the dark. Also, if she was a vampire, she couldn't be outside during the day… even one with dense rain clouds.

I signaled for her to wait before turning and darting over to the bedroom door. We didn't have a lock on the door, but I took the chair from my desk and wedged the top of it under the doorknob. I didn't think that would really hold back any determined effort to open the door, but it would at least give me fair warning if my parents or brother tried to get into the room.

While my back was turned, I didn't like knowing that Sylvia was watching me. It gave me a creepy feeling between my shoulder blades. But I also tried to convince myself I was imagining this. When I turned back around, she would be gone.

But… again… no.

When I turned and faced the window, she was still there. Her hair and the thin nightgown she was wearing were soaked through. I could see the outlines of her body through the sheer white material. She looked thin… undernourished, but I also couldn't help but notice the curves of her body. They had an effect on me that made me uncomfortable.

I was shaking inside and out as I walked slowly back to my bed and knelt down on it, facing her. After casting a wary glance over my shoulder, I reached up and unlocked the window. There was a weird twisting sensation in my stomach, like it was filled with a nest of snakes as I placed the heels of my hands under the top edge of the window and started to push up.

The wood was swollen from the dampness, and it yielded slowly, making what to me, anyway, was an ear-piercing shriek as the window frame slid in the track. As soon as there was an opening, wind and rainwater gusted in with a sizzling hiss. I struggled to get the window halfway up, and when I couldn't make it go any further, I leaned down and stuck my face into the three-inch opening.

The cool dampness of the storm speckled my face as if Sylvia wasn't even there to block it. I had to crane my head to one side so I could look up at her. She shifted her position and brought her face down to the opening, close to mine. Only the screen and maybe three or four inches separated us. I had the crazy notion that we were going to kiss, but we didn't.

"What are you doing up here?" I asked. It took a lot of effort to keep my voice down low so no one downstairs would hear me, but I also had to speak loud enough so she could hear me above the howling wind.

"I came to see you," she said in that lilting, airy whisper of hers.

"But why? How'd you get up on the roof?"

There have been plenty of nights when, late at night, I'd sneak out onto the roof outside my window. Sometimes I would jump down to the ground and run off to meet up with some friends to run around the neighborhood, but there were more nights than I could count when I would just sit up there on the roof, lean against the house, and look up at the stars and imagine all sorts of things.

She didn't answer me, and I was perplexed. There was no way she could have put a ladder up against the house and climbed up. The wind would have whisked it and her away. So unless she jumped or flew up here, she must have climbed and scrambled up somehow. I had tried climbing up my mother's rose trellis once, but I ended up breaking it. And once, when I stood on a chair and jumped up, I couldn't pull myself over the rain gutters. I doubted she had the strength to do something like that.

"I've been really worried about you," I said, deciding not to press her on how she got up onto the roof. "Where'd you spend the night?"

"My home is… gone."

When she said that, her voice caught, and I noticed the brief glance she shot over her shoulder in what I assumed was the direction of her home or at least the house where she was staying.

"Did the storm destroy it?"

"My home is gone," was all she said again, and the wistful tone in her voice all but broke my heart.

"Where are you staying, then? Who are you staying with?"

"I've been outside since it happened."

"In this storm? Your parents must be worried about you. They must be out looking for you."

She slid her lower lip under her teeth and bit down, making it go bone white. Rain was streaming down her face. I was sure it was mixed with tears. The whites of her eyes were red-rimmed, and I wondered—again—if she might be a vampire.

"I don't have any parents," she finally said.

"You mean they… died?"

She nodded.

"Who do you live with, then? An aunt or uncle? A grandparent?"

Again, she cast a wary glance over her shoulder. She looked like she was expecting someone or something terrible to sneak up behind her.

"I've been outside ever since that happened," she said.

I was getting tired of her repeating herself like that, and I was nervous, worrying that my brother or one of my parents would come upstairs and find me talking to a girl hanging around outside my window.

This is insane, I thought, but I went ahead and said what I was thinking anyway.

"Do you need someplace to stay?"

She didn't answer me right away, and I listened to my heart thumping in my ears. The pulse was so strong it made my wrists ache. The rain sluiced against the window, whipping her across the back like a bullwhip. I was desperate, wondering what if anything I could do to help.

"You have to come in here, then," I finally said.

I shifted so I could put more effort into trying to open the window. Kneeling on the bed, I pressed the palms of my hands against the window frame and, gritting my teeth, pushed with everything I had. The window moved, but not far. It sent a weird vibrating hum through the window frame. The lead weights inside the frame started banging like ancient gongs.

Slowly… slowly the window rose until it stuck about three-quarters of the way up. After that, no matter how hard I pushed, I couldn't get it to go the rest of the way. I was worried that I might have as much trouble getting it back down, but I'd deal with that when and if it happened. I fumbled to unlatch the screen and was running it up when footsteps sounded on the stairs.

"*Shit!*" I muttered, making sure I didn't say it loud enough for anyone to hear in case it was my mother or father.

I wheeled around as the bedroom doorknob started to turn. The chair was propped against the door, but I knew it wouldn't stop whoever was out there. I looked back outside at Sylvia. She had obviously heard the footsteps, too, although I have no idea how over the sounds of the storm.

She stood up quickly and then, with a last, lingering look at me, jumped up into the air. Her bare feet were the last thing I saw as she disappeared above my window. I cringed, waiting to see her fall from the rooftop, but she didn't.

She was gone … just like *that!*
Gone!

"What the heck're you doing?" Bobby asked as he pushed the door open, knocking the desk chair over so it clattered onto the floor.

I turned and looked at him wide-eyed. All I wanted to do was look outside to see what had happened to Sylvia. It was impossible that she had jumped up on to the roof of the main house, but where else could she have gone. Maybe she was a really good jumper, and that's how she got up onto the utility room roof in the first place, but how could she keep her balance on the roof in weather like this?

None of it made any sense, but I couldn't mention to Bobby what had just happened.

He'd say I was crazy, and then give me a punch in the gut for good measure.

But I couldn't just leave Sylvia out there.

If she really had jumped onto the roof of the main house, she couldn't stay there. She'd slip and fall, and then how would I explain a dead girl or a girl with a broken back or legs lying on the ground close to the house?

"Are you nuts?" Bobby shouted.

It took me a moment to realize he was talking about the wide open window. Rain was blowing in, and droplets were running across the top of the screen like beads of quicksilver. Then I realized that my bed and I were getting soaked from the spray. Shaking my head and muttering something that didn't make sense, I ran the screen down and then started trying to pull the window down. At first, it didn't budge, but then—with effort—I got it to go down. At the very end, it slipped fast and slammed shut with a resounding boom that almost broke the glass.

"Just… you know… ahh… looking at the storm."

Bobby regarded me with a skeptical look. Then he shook his head and plopped down on his bed.

"Everything okay up there?" my mother shouted from downstairs.

"We're fine," I yelled so she would know Bobby wasn't beating me up and come upstairs.

"You're nuts, you know that?" Bobby said from his bed.

I shrugged, half-expecting him to leap off the bed and punch me, but he grabbed a *Turok Son of Stone* comic book from the bookshelf next to his bed and settled down to read.

I stared at him for the longest time, not knowing what to say or do next, but I was dying to look outside again to see where Sylvia had gone. All I could think was, what I had just witnessed was impossible. I had a single mental image seared into my brain that made me so sick with worry I was nauseous. All I could imagine was Sylvia, her wet hair and nightgown clinging to her body as she crouched on the peak of the roof and cried as the hurricane roared around her.

TEN

Late in the afternoon, the storm finally began to weaken. The winds stopped howling and came in fitful gusts that every now and then still packed a wallop. The rain was no longer coming at the house almost horizontally. Overhead, the clouds were still thick and as dark as soot, but there was a feeling in the air that told me it was all but over.

The problem was I didn't feel the tiniest bit of relief. If anything, I was more worried. I couldn't stop thinking about Sylvia and wondering where she was and what she was doing. Had she gotten down off the roof, or was she still up there, maybe afraid to climb down?

Of course, all of my speculation rested on whether or not she was real in the first place.

I didn't see how she could have survived the night out in the storm.

And how in the name of God could she have jumped up onto the top roof of the house?

Even if she somehow clambered up onto the

utility room roof, there was no way what I saw after that had really happened.

Telling my mother I was checking out the storm damage, I went from room to room, upstairs and down, and looked outside, but I didn't see her anywhere. That didn't mean she wasn't out there somewhere—maybe sprawled facedown and lifeless in the wet grass and mud. I just couldn't see her. I was desperate to go outside and make sure she wasn't there, but there was no way my folks would let me go outside… not yet, anyway. Maybe in the morning, once the storm was truly gone. No doubt, my father was going to make me and Bobby help him clean up the mess in the yard. For now, though, all I could do was fret about Sylvia and wonder—if she was even real—where she was now.

Throughout the day and into the evening, my mother picked up that something was bothering me. Over and over, she asked me what it was, but I wouldn't tell her. I was tempted to, but I didn't because, as evening came, I began to worry about something else.

I was worried that the whole thing might have been a hallucination… that I might be losing my mind and imagining things. I had to figure out some way of knowing that Sylvia was real.

My family had spent the day looking for things to do. My mother, especially, wanted to do something as a family, but we ended up pretty much getting on everyone else's nerves. My mom busied herself in the kitchen because, without electricity, she couldn't run the vacuum through the house. My dad spent lots of time down in the cellar looking for leaks and listening to the weather forecast on his transistor radio. He kept yelling up the latest reports on the storm, but it all sounded the same to me—wind and rain.

My brother and I got into a few squabbles… Nothing I started, of course. He wanted to work on his model cars, but with the power still out, the lighting was so bad he couldn't see to work. That made him edgy. My mother exploded at him when he suggested he could use a couple of candles.

"That glue is flammable!" she yelled. Even at the time, I remember thinking that she had overreacted about such a simple request. Years later, though, when she was in the nursing home, she told me how when she was young, her baby brother had died in a house fire. For the rest of her life, the thought of her house burning down terrified her. Which explained why I had such a fear of fire – even though she had never said anything to me about it.

Of course, Bobby took out his irritability by sniping at me, but I was too stressed out to rise to the bait. This made it not as much fun for him, so he had left me alone for most of the day.

I sat on my bed reading until daylight began to fail. As always, I kept looking out at the Big Tree and onto the roof to see if I could catch a glimpse of Sylvia. I was more and more convinced she had to have been imaginary, like the monster my cousin Jean was afraid of. The monster's name was "Big Bad," and he lived in Jean's bedroom closet. He could only get out if the closet door was left open, even a little bit, so Jean made sure—every night—to close it and put something in front of it to block it shut or wake her up if Big Bad tried to get out.

Finally—when night came, I was grateful to go to bed early. My father's periodic reports from the basement: "No leaks down here yet," and "Supposed to be over by morning," had kept me up to date. I felt like we had been caged up in the house for weeks. I figured we would have at least one more day off from school, at least until the electricity was restored, but my father reported that they'd announced on the radio that school would open in the morning, as usual.

That was a relief.

Of course, my sleep that night was interrupted so many times I lost count. I couldn't tell if they were dreams or real or something in that in-between state, like that TV show my folks wouldn't let me watch— *The Twilight Zone*. I certainly felt as though I didn't sleep at all, and time and again, I would "wake up" to find myself sitting up in bed, leaning on the windowsill, and staring out at what was left of the Big Tree. There were a few times I was sure I saw *something* moving around down there, but I never caught a glimpse of Sylvia, and I began to worry that I would never see her again.

Dawn came on slowly, turning the sky sooty gray. Then faint pink lines appeared in the East. Soft pastels gradually changed to bright lines of electric red and orange that looked like forks of lightning, frozen against the receding clouds. Once I was positive I was truly awake, I felt a deep relief, knowing that the storm was over. At some point, someone—I assumed my mother—started banging around downstairs. Without thinking, I reached for the reading lamp next to my bed and flicked the switch. I let out a grunt of surprise when the light came on. The power was back.

"Crap," I whispered.

I turned and brought my face so close to the

closed window that when I sighed, my breath fogged the glass. This meant—for sure—there would be school today. That was a relief, but it also meant that I wouldn't be able to check out the Big Tree until after school. There was no way I could get outside now, not with my mother up and about.

"Boys…"

My mother's voice echoing in the stairwell made me jump.

"Time to get up and get ready for school!"

"Be right down," I called out.

I decided to get dressed before going downstairs for breakfast. Maybe I'd get a chance to get out and look for Sylvia, if only for a few minutes, before I had to leave for school.

"Well, look at you, already dressed and ready to start the day," my mother said when she saw me. I made a habit of not getting dressed until after breakfast. My father even joked that I'd go to school wearing my pajamas if I could get away with it. I wolfed down my oatmeal and gulped my orange juice, hoping to sneak out, but my father was dressed and ready to go early.

"Come on boys, I'll give you a ride to school," he said. He was impatient to get to the office, having missed two days of work, and there was probably a thousand things waiting for him as a result of the storm damage. So I had to get in the car without going over to the Big Tree. Of course Bobby sat in the front seat, like always.

~ * ~

School was school. Everyone was talking about what they had done and what had happened during the hurricane. Kids had stories about branches coming down on their yards and bursting through windows, trees and light poles falling down, a few lobster boats coming off their moorings and getting washed ashore, but—thank God—nobody had died, and no one suffered any catastrophic losses except for Old Man O'Connell, whose garage was flattened when a tree landed on it. Both Jimmy and Ray said they were disappointed there hadn't been more destruction, but on their way to school, they had both seen that the tree house had come crashing down.

"Don't sweat it," Jimmy said. "We'll build it again and make it even better." He had decided to forget about me punching him, which was a relief.

Whenever we had a chance to talk—like at lunch or recess—I tried to work up the courage to tell my friends about Sylvia. In the clear light of day, though, my memory of her was rapidly fading, and I became increasingly convinced that I had dreamed or imagined her.

Maybe I was going crazy. I was so wound up— "as tight as a tick," my mother often said—that even my friends noticed. Jimmy asked me a couple of times what was wrong. When I told him nothing, he shook his head and said he could tell I was lying. Several times throughout the day, I'd catch him staring at me in class like I was a specimen under a microscope. When we made eye contact, he would lower his gaze and shake his head.

I couldn't stop thinking about Sylvia and worrying

about her… about if she was real, that is.

All of the adults in town, I was sure, would be taking time off from work today to clean up their yards and do whatever repairs needed doing. I was positive that, sooner or later, Walt was going to get out his chainsaw and axe, and start cutting up the branches that had fallen off the Big Tree. I tried not to think the worst, but I convinced myself that he was going to take it one step further and cut down the whole thing, now that it had been destroyed.

School dragged on… as usual, and by the time two-thirty rolled around, I was raring to get home and see what was going on. When the bell rang, I didn't even wait for Jimmy or Ray to come outside. I just ran as fast as I could. I heard one of my friends—I think it was Jimmy—call out for me to wait up, but I was already up the hill and out of sight, heading for home.

As I jogged onto the last turn in the road before the straightaway to my house, I heard a sound that chilled me—a low, irregular buzzing, sputtering sound that I knew right away had to be a chainsaw. Horrible images flashed through my mind, and my heart started slamming like a jackhammer in my chest. I raced as fast as I could. As I got closer, the sound grew louder, and I saw a cloud of blue smoke drifting lazily across the street in front of Old Lady Wayrenen's house.

"God, *no!*" I shouted. My heart was wedged into my throat. My hands were greasy with sweat. Up ahead, parked on the side of the road, halfway onto Old Lady Wayrenen's yard, was Jimmy's Uncle Walt's dump truck. It was half-filled with thick branches and the cracked and broken boards of our tree house. Already, the leaves were wilting and fluttering in the faint breeze.

I stopped a few feet from the truck and, leaning over to catch my breath, stared in absolute horror.

Walt had already finished trimming most of the branches. He'd cut them so they'd fit into the high-walled bed of the dump truck. I figured he would take them back to his house and cut and split them for firewood. But now—

I couldn't believe it!

—he was cutting a huge wedge into the side of the Big Tree a few feet above ground level.

The work was going slowly. His chainsaw bucked and whined in his hands as it bit into the old wood. The sound set my teeth on edge as I watched a fountain of wheat-colored sawdust arc into the air.

The Big Tree was done for.

Walt noticed me standing there on the side of the street and stopped cutting. With his chainsaw still crackling and burring at his side, he looked at me and waved.

Finding it almost impossible to raise my arm, I waved back. It felt like my arm was being controlled by a puppet's string.

Walt smiled broadly, his teeth looking particularly bright in his tanned face. He seemed to genuinely like us kids even though we tormented him and his horses something wicked and had no qualms about raiding his or any other neighbor's garden once they started to yield. Walt's face was streaked with sweat, and his work clothes were dirty and covered with twigs, sawdust, and pitch. Blackened leaves clung to his clothes like bloated leeches. His bare forearms were covered with sawdust.

"How's things?" he called out, shouting so I could

hear him over the rattling, sputtering noise his chainsaw was making.

I shrugged, wishing to God I had the courage to speak up to an adult and ask or tell him or *beg* him, if I had to, *not* to cut down the Big Tree.

Sure, it was wounded, but it didn't have to die!

"Sorry 'bout your tree house," he said.

I shrugged as tears filled my eyes as I picked up my backpack and took off running for our driveway. My leg muscles felt like rubber as I slowed my pace and walked into the yard. The chainsaw started growling again, and, turning, I saw that Walt had resumed his work. Jimmy, trailing behind me, had stopped like I had and was watching his uncle wreak havoc on what to my way of thinking was the most important thing in our lives.

Jimmy saw me looking at him and waved. I waved back, but when he waved me over, I didn't move. I wanted to make it clear that I didn't want to talk to him or anybody else. Even at a distance, as the blue smoke from the chainsaw and spray of sawdust rose into the air, the sound of the chainsaw hurt my ears.

It was the sound of doom.

But beneath that sound, I gradually became aware of something else… another sound.

I wasn't sure when I had started to hear it. Once I noticed, it seemed like it had been there all along, even when I was at school today. It was simply that I hadn't been conscious of it until now.

It was faint and almost impossible to hear above the roar of Walt's chainsaw, but once I knew it was there, I struggled to focus on it. I couldn't tell what direction it was coming from. It seemed to originate from several directions at once, but finally I turned toward the backyard, and I knew—somehow—that it was coming from the woods behind our house.

Feeling like I was moving in a dream, I started walking across the back lawn, lured by the sound. As I did, the sound—a faint moaning mixed with stifled cries of either pain or grief—grew louder.

The back boundary of our yard was a wooded area that sloped down into low-lying wetlands we all called "The Swamp." It wasn't a large area of woods—certainly not worthy of the name "forest." Only an acre or two. But my friends and I played there when the ground was dry, usually in mid-summer. We built huts from branches and shot our bows and arrows, pretending to be Robin Hood and his Merry Men or fierce Mohawk Indians. But now, as I started across the lawn toward the woods, I saw them differently.

They looked deeper and darker than I had ever imagined, and I could all but feel… something… a strange, possibly dangerous presence lurking somewhere in the shaded depths, watching me, trying to lure me there.

As frightening as that idea was, I didn't hesitate.

The backyard was littered with blown-down leaves and branches, but none of the trees, not even the birches had fallen. As I moved across the lawn heading toward the woods, I picked up my pace until I was running.

As I ran, the tone of the sound I had been hearing changed subtly. It began to sound desperate, and it was punctuated by shrill shrieks of what I could only think was genuine panic and pain.

The air became chilly as I started into the woods, following one of the many trails my friends and I had worn into the turf. Goose bumps sprinkled my arms, and I cringed as the wailing sound grew steadily louder. The roar of Walt's chainsaw faded into the distance until it was a faraway white noise, and it seemed as if as one melted away, the other rose in intensity.

Someone's hurt!

Someone's in pain!

Someone's dying!

The only thought in my mind was that it might be Sylvia.

If she had spent the night outside like she said, she had to have stayed somewhere. She could have tried hiding in our garage, I thought, but my father had locked it up tight before the storm. Maybe she knew about the huts we had built out in "The Swamp" and had tried to spend the night in one of them.

The winding trail was covered with blown-down leaves and branches, and the ground was soggy underfoot. A couple of times, my foot got sucked down into the mud, and once I almost lost my sneaker when I pulled it out. The footing wasn't very good, either. The mud was as slippery, as if the ground had been oiled. Although I wasn't sure where I was going—the sound still seemed to be coming from several directions at once—I kept running, slipping and sliding as I went.

I drew to a sudden stop, though, when I arrived at a spot where my friends and I often played—a small clearing that was surrounded by several beech trees. What few leaves remained were yellowed by the approach of autumn. Branches had snapped off during the storm.

At first, I thought the clearing was empty, but then my eyes adjusted, and I saw Sylvia crouched at the far edge of the clearing. She was shaded by the trees and blended into the scenery like she was wearing camouflage. Her head was bowed as she stared down at the leaf-covered ground. Her pale skin was dappled with beams of sunlight that made it look like she'd been caught in a shower of golden coins.

But there were also lines that looked like dark splashes of ink on her skin. Even then, I knew that they weren't shadows, but my mind refused to process what I was seeing.

"Sylvia," I called out.

My voice wasn't much more than a bullfrog croak, and for the longest time, she didn't look up. I wasn't sure she knew I was there, and I didn't want to startle her. Thinking she hadn't heard me, I called her name again but still got no response.

She looked like an illusion, and I was afraid that she was going to disappear as soon as I tried to approach her.

Before I could call her name a third time, she raised her head slowly and looked up at me. The faintest of smiles shifted across her face, but then, in an instant, the corners of her mouth were dragged down into a horrible grimace as something dark and red flowed from her mouth and dripped onto her chest and arms. She shrieked, loudly, and gripped herself in intense pain. Then, her eyes glistening with silver fire, she leaned her head back so she was looking up at the sky.

"What is it?" I cried, my voice warbling. "What's the matter?"

She didn't say a word or utter a sound, but only

for a moment. I was vaguely aware of the sound of Walt's chainsaw far off in the distance, but when that sound rose in intensity, Sylvia let out a piercing scream as dark streaks sliced across her skin.

I knew, then, that she was bleeding and, somehow, I connected it with the distant sound of Walt's chainsaw.

"What's wrong?" I asked even though on some level I already knew.

"He's destroying my home," she said.

Her voice was low and soft, but the whisper was far from savage or angry. It was filled with loss and anguish. The sound of it filled me with almost overwhelming sadness.

From far away, the rattling roar of the chainsaw rose higher. I turned and looked in its direction, but it was impossible to see where the Big Tree used to stand.

"They've taken my home," Sylvia said. "I've got nowhere to go."

The truth was slowly dawning on me, but I couldn't believe it. I had read Greek mythology, and I knew about forest nymphs and other sylvan creatures that supposedly lived in the woods, but I always thought they were make-believe. When my friends and I played out here in the woods and pretended we were English outlaws or savage Indians, we knew on some level that we were pretending even though a part of us was convinced we really *were* outlaws or Indians.

I jumped when Sylvia sucked in a deep breath and, wincing in pain, leaned her head back and, looking up, let out a screech that froze me where I stood. And then, before I could blink, much less do anything to stop it, a deep, red slash appeared across her throat. The scream cut off with a loud bubbling sound, and she slumped forward, falling face-first onto the leaf-strewn ground.

As afraid and confused as I was, I somehow found the strength to move toward her. I was shaking as I knelt at her side and saw what I hadn't been able to see clearly when she was sitting in the shade. Her body was covered with dozens… hundreds of slices. Blood so red it looked black in the gloom of the woods welled up from her wounds, glistening like ruby-tinged oil as it ran down her face and arms, and spilled onto the ground.

My heart was pounding, and my breath was raw and hot in my throat as I stared at her in disbelief. I had no idea what to do even though I was desperate to do whatever I could to try to save her.

But I knew, even then, I couldn't stop it.

She was dying.

I reached out and touched her gently on the shoulder. She rolled over onto her back and looked up at me with one eye opened to a mere slit. Her body shivered and shuddered as blood spewed from her wounds. I hoped that she was already past feeling any pain.

I wanted to believe that, but the way she twitched and thrashed as more bloody gashes appeared on her body told me otherwise.

"Don't die," I whispered even though I already knew it was futile. "Please. Don't die."

There was nothing I could do.

As much as I wanted to do something—anything—to help her, I had no idea what other than try to comfort her.

My mind was a roaring blank as I knelt beside her and looked around. The trees pressed in around me, seeming to trap me where I was. The chainsaw was still roaring in the distance, and even though a small voice told me that it was already too late, I knew I had to try to stop it. Standing up and wheeling around, I started running back to my house and to Walt with his chainsaw.

My feet splashed in puddles and slipped on the mud-slick trail as I ran for all I was worth. The wind tore into my lungs, and branches lashed my face and arms as bitter tears streamed from my eyes. Fear and anger and panic possessed me in a way I have never experienced either before or since. My feet pounded the wet ground, making my vision jump with every step. It seemed to take forever, but eventually I broke out of the woods and raced across my backyard.

Suddenly, everything seemed to shift into slow motion. Jimmy was still standing in the street, watching his uncle cut up the Big Tree. The roaring of the chainsaw was so loud it blotted out everything else... even my voice when I started yelling, "No! Don't! Stop it!"

For what seemed like forever, neither Walt nor Jimmy seemed to notice me. The image of Sylvia's bloody, crumpled body rose up in my mind.

"Stop it! Please!" I shouted as loud as I could.

My heart was pounding so hard I thought it was going to burst out of my chest.

"You're killing her! You're killing her!"

Even as I said those words, the rattling burr of the chainsaw stopped. I saw the huge wedge that was cut into the side of the Big Tree. Walt had been cutting into the opposite side, taking out smaller chunks as he went. He stepped back and stopped his chainsaw.

I knew that the Big Tree had reached its limit.

The sudden stillness lasted only a few seconds. Then the most horrific snapping, cracking, tearing sound filled the air as the wood in the core—the heartwood of the Big Tree—finally gave way.

The Big Tree began to fall.

"*No!*" I shrieked as the sound grew louder, like a string of dynamite going off. The upper branches shifted to one side and then started to fall in a slow sweep that raked the sky. More branches lower down snapped as the bulk of the Big Tree toppled over and hit the ground with a resounding boom that shook the earth so much I could feel it in my feet.

My voice twisted off into a squeak when I saw that it was too late. The Big Tree was down. If it had ever been Sylvia's home, it wasn't now.

"Cool!" I heard someone say behind me.

I turned and saw my brother, standing on the edge of our driveway, watching what was happening. The grin on his face made him look like an idiot. My body tensed, ready for the jab as he came closer to me. Tears were running in hot, wet lines down both my cheeks. When he stopped beside me and looked at me, his voice was thick with mockery when he said, "Look at you, crying like a little baby."

I snapped.

Clenching my hand into a fist I imagined was as round and hard as a rock, I spun around on one foot and, uttering the wildest, loudest cry I have ever made, drove it into the pit of his stomach.

The air came out of him in a single loud *whoosh* as my fist buried itself into his belly. His eyes widened so much they nearly popped out of his head, and he let out a horrific groan as he doubled over and then, in slow motion, dropped to his knees. I didn't realize it until later, but when he hit the ground, his teeth clacked together and snipped off the tip of his tongue. For the rest of his life, Bobby spoke with a slight lisp.

I had no idea what I was doing. I was blinded by fury and panic and grief. I watched in amazement as my brother pitched backward onto the ground, hitting the back of his head hard. My first lucid thought was that I had killed him, but then I saw that his eyes were open and his chest was heaving up and down. For what seemed like the longest time but was probably actually only a few seconds, he lay sprawled on his back on the ground. His eyelids fluttered crazily, like he was trying to blink away tears. Then, wincing through his pain, he shifted his eyes and glared at me.

He mumbled something, but I couldn't make out what he said. I had no doubt it was something like: "I'm gonna kill you!" but his voice was bubbly with blood and mucous.

But that wasn't what set me off.

No.

What threw me into a fury was the look he gave me. Even though he was down on the ground, he looked at me like he had won. He smiled at me, and that smile... that irksome damned smile of his made something inside me snap. I winced as if whatever had snapped had been audible. Uttering a cry that seemed to tear through me from the bottom of my gut, I leaped into the air and landed on him.

Hard.

The impact forced an explosion of air from his lungs. I caught a whiff of his breath as it blew into my face. It smelled like rotten eggs. Even that tiny sensation fueled my sudden rage. Pinning his shoulders down with my knees, I sat on his chest and began to pummel him with both fists raining down on him in a blur... a blur of which I—apparently—was the center.

I'm the eye of the hurricane, I thought, forgetting for a moment that the eye of a hurricane is the calmest spot, not the wildest.

I can honestly say that I was out of my mind. Ever since that day, I can understand when people who have committed a crime plead temporary insanity. I kept punching my brother until his face was so smeared with blood it looked like he'd mashed raspberry jelly all over it. I was all the more infuriated when his nose made a loud cracking sound, and thick, red flows of blood that looked like thick strands of red ribbon gushed out. When he took a shallow breath and exhaled, a fine mist of blood sprayed my face.

My fists felt like they were on fire, and I was breathing with a mighty roar with every inhalation. There was a small part of me that was perfectly clear and at peace, like I was sitting outside myself, watching as I developed a cadence, punching and punching, releasing years of pent-up anger at being bullied all the time.

I became vaguely aware that Walt and Jimmy were standing behind me, watching me in amazement. I could hear myself talking—yelling, truth be told as I pummeled my brother.

"You *did* it! ...You *all* did it! ...You *killed* her! ...You *killed* her!"

That's as much as I can remember saying. I'm sure

I hollered and screamed all sorts of things… terrible things that wouldn't make sense to anyone except me because no one else knew about Sylvia.

But I did, and I was sure she was dead… that cutting down the tree had killed her. Every cut into the Big Tree had taken away her home… her source of life.

But those were thoughts I didn't have at the time. They came much later, after I had calmed down and had plenty of time to think it over. And I had plenty because of what happened next.

I was completely swept up by my rage when I felt something hard and powerful clamp down on my shoulder from behind. Without even thinking, I shifted forward, got my legs under me, and then spun around as I stood up. My fist was clenched, and I swung it as hard as I could. Before I could stop myself, my fist hit Walt in the face, just below his left eye socket.

It was like hitting a brick wall. The pain in my hand was so intense and so immediate I was sure I'd crushed every bone in my hand. What was worse, though, was the look of total surprise on Walt's face as he stepped back and raised his arms to shield himself in case I kept up my assault. When I didn't, he lowered his guard and placed one hand over the spot where I'd hit him. His blue eyes gleamed over the back of his work-tanned hand.

"Damn," was all he said, and I thought I saw a smile flicker across his face. "You got one helluva punch."

I would never be sure if he was mad or proud of me because at that precise moment, I heard footsteps coming up behind me. I turned to see my mother, charging across the driveway to the scene of the crime.

And what a crime it was.

It was bad enough that I had beat on Bobby so badly, but I had done something much worse. I had actually hauled off and punched an adult in the face.

I was dead, and I knew it.

"What the devil is going on here?" my mother shouted.

Her eyes flashed with anger and surprise when she looked at Bobby, who only now was sitting up and wiping blood from his nose. He was trembling as he got slowly to his feet. His lower face was a dripping mask of blood, and his eyes were glazed as though he was still stunned and confused by my sudden furious retaliation. He wiped his mouth and nose with both hands, also stained with blood.

When he spoke, I couldn't make out anything he said, but that may have been because of the loud whooshing sound in my ears. Apparently my mother understood him because she turned to face me, her face pale with shock. Her eyes were so wide they looked like golf balls stuck in her face.

"Did you really?" she asked. Her voice was as harsh and loud as the Trumpet of Doom.

"Did I what?" I asked.

I was shaking in my sneakers, but I fought to maintain control. My fists were throbbing from the pummeling I'd given Bobby—and Walt. I could feel Walt's glare boring into my back as I stared back at my mother.

I was at a complete loss for words. If I told her or anyone the truth—that I was furious because Walt had cut down Sylvia's house and killed her—they would have taken me off to the loony bin in Danvers. But if I lied, anyone—especially my mother—would see it on my face and hear it in my voice.

"Did you really hit Mr. Wayrenen?"

"It was nothing," Walt said, definitely smiling now. "I just caught one on the chin when I was trying to break it up. It was an accident, right?"

He looked at me and winked, but I was dumbfounded. I couldn't believe he was lying or, if not outright lying, at least distorting the truth to protect me. My mother didn't say anything for the longest time. Bobby, meanwhile, was standing close beside her, looking a lot smaller to me now. Like me, he was trying not to sob, but he was obviously in a great deal of pain. His shoulders were jerking up and down like he was crying as he hunched forward and kept wiping his face.

"And you beat up your brother?" she said.

I wasn't sure if that was a question or a statement of fact. Probably both, but either way, there was no way I could deny it... not with Walt and Jimmy standing there as witnesses. I wasn't an adult. I couldn't lie and get away with it.

So what could I do?

I nodded, trying my best not to look my mother straight in the eyes. She had an uncanny way of making me think— no, not "think"—know that she could tell whether or not I was lying whenever I spoke. It was like some freaky gift.

"He was teasing me," I finally said, my voice low and meek. When I glanced at the blood on Bobby's face, I realized just how doomed I was.

"Teasing you?" my mother said, echoing what I'd said with an odd, neutral tone.

"Uh-huh… like he always does, and I just couldn't take it anymore."

I was so close to tears my eyes felt like they'd been bathed in acid, but I told myself that I couldn't cry… not here… not in front of Jimmy and Walt and, worst of all, my brother. I had to be content that I had won. I had finally gotten Bobby back for all those years of torment and misery he had inflicted on me, not just physically, but psychologically, as well.

"What was he teasing you about?"

I sniffed and then clamped my jaw shut tight because there was no way I was going to say why. It might lead me to say exactly why.

"I was upset because… because Walt was cutting… cutting down the Big Tree."

My mother crossed her arms over her chest and was silent for the longest time as she stared at me. Finally, she said one of the absolute worst things a kid can ever hear:

"Just you wait until your father gets home, young man."

I'm dead was all I could think. When I took a breath, it whistled in my throat.

"Go to your room, and don't you *dare* come downstairs until I call you."

With nothing to do or say, I trudged across the lawn to the front door and went inside, leaving everyone else behind.

ELEVEN

There's no way I could begin to describe what I was feeling as I lay on my bed and waited for my father to get home. Even though I put my pillow over my face to block out the world, I could still hear Walt's chainsaw as he cut up what was left of the Big Tree into smaller pieces that would fit into the bed of his dump truck. I didn't even care that he was taking the lumber we'd used to build the tree house. It certainly wasn't as intense as Sylvia had felt it, but each cut sent a razor-like chill through me. At that exact moment, I knew that an essential part of my childhood had come to an end, never to return.

At some point late in the afternoon, my brother came upstairs, but he only went to the bathroom and didn't even stay in there all that long. He must really be hurting, I thought, if he doesn't want to fiddle with himself. A little after five o'clock, my father got home from work. I heard his car pull into the driveway, and I jumped when he slammed the car door behind him when he got out. I was sweating in expectation of what was to come…

Soon!

Tossing my pillow aside, I rolled off my bed and went to the bedroom door, opening it a crack so I could hear anything my folks said downstairs. Mostly, I heard my mother's voice, buzzing indistinctly as she and my dad moved about in the kitchen and she told him about what I had done. I considered sneaking down the stairs like I often did to eavesdrop on them, but I knew how badly it would go for me if I got caught. Sooner or later—and it would be sooner, I feared—my father was going to come upstairs and dole out my punishment.

I caught fragments of what they were saying. At one point, my father asked if he should talk to Walt and get his version of the story, but my mother said all he had to do was look at Bobby's face to know how serious this was. My father called Bobby into the kitchen from the living room where he was—uncharacteristically—*not* watching TV. I imagined he had been sitting there, sulking or, more likely, anxiously awaiting my father so I would get what was coming to me.

Their voices rose a bit louder once Bobby joined them. After what could only have been thirty or so seconds even though it seemed much longer, my father's footsteps sounded in the stairwell.

I dropped back onto my bed and lay down with my face to the wall. I was frantic to try to come up with some kind of defense, but my mind was a blank. All I could think was, above all else, I could *never* tell him the truth about Sylvia.

He knocked lightly on my door before turning the doorknob and entering. Even that little detail—

that he knocked before entering—let me know that I was in serious, serious trouble.

"Come in," I said, even though I knew he had already entered the bedroom. I tried to look small on my bed, hoping he would take pity on me and not belt me the way he did sometimes when I really screwed up.

"So what's this I hear about you punching Mr. Wayrenen?"

I lay there with my back to him, frantically searching for something to say and, more importantly, hoping to control my voice so he wouldn't hear how scared I was.

"Turn around and look at me when I'm talking to you," he said, a bit more harshly.

I don't know where I found the strength to roll over, but I did. I was so close to crying I knew I was going to break before this was over. I almost hoped my father would give me a spanking so, like he sometimes said, he could "give me something to cry about."

"I didn't mean to do it," I said in a low, shattered voice.

"What's that? I didn't hear you."

I knew he had heard me. He wanted to see me squirm when I had to say it again.

"I *said* I didn't *mean* to!"

"So why'd you do it?"

He had me there. I had calmed down now, but I could still recall all too clearly the pitch of anger I experienced when Bobby said something about me crying. Thinking about it now, it was probably a good thing Walt pulled me off Bobby when he did because I really might have seriously hurt my brother or maybe even killed him. As much as I said I hated Bobby and as much as I was convinced he genuinely hated me, I sure didn't want to murder him... not really.

"I don't know," I finally said, knowing even before the words were out of my mouth that my excuse wasn't going to wash. My father seemed to be enjoying making me twist in the wind like this. Again, I almost longed for a beating just so I could get the whole thing over with.

"I saw what you did to Bobby," my father said. Now that the knife was in, he was turning it. "You hurt him bad."

Not as bad as he hurt me, I wanted to say, but I offered no response. Even now that I had calmed down, I didn't feel bad about hurting Bobby. I couldn't stop remembering how many times—pretty much every day—he hit or poked or jabbed or punched me. I'd finally had enough, and I had snapped. Was that a good defense? I doubted that my father could or even wanted to understand how I was feeling. He'd had a brother and sister, and I knew—intellectually—that he had been a kid at one time, but I certainly couldn't imagine him as a child, and he sure didn't seem like someone who would understand what it was like growing up with a bully for a brother. Like always, I expected that he would tell me I'd have to toughen up if I was going to make my way in the world.

"You're gonna have to apologize to Mr. Wayrenen," he said. "Your mom was thinking of making you write him an apology, but I say you have to deal with this like a man and apologize to him, face to face."

His words hit me like I was being speared by an

iron bar. I'd had to do something like that once before. When I was six, I had stolen three pieces of penny candy from the corner store. When my mother found out—I have no idea how she found out, by the way. Bobby probably squealed on me—my father traipsed me down to the store and made me apologize to Mr. Arugo, the old Italian who ran the store. I also, of course, had to pay for the candy. Mr. Arugo had said at the time that he would have to keep a special eye on me after that, but in truth, he treated me more kindly and, from time to time, even slipped an extra piece of candy into my bag. He'd wink to let me know that he knew what he had done.

But this… this was going to be hell. Walt had killed the Big Tree. He had killed Sylvia.

But I determined then and there to keep it simple. I'd apologize for punching him, and I'd hope that would be enough because the truth was, I wasn't at all sorry. I certainly wasn't sorry that I beat up on Bobby, and as scared as I was, I wasn't sorry that I hit Walt when he tried to stop me from pummeling my brother. The truth was, I was glad I had hit Walt.

"Do you hear me?" my father said.

Lost as I was in thought, I nodded, unable to speak.

"All right, then. Let's go."

He took a deep breath and let it out slowly. I tensed, thinking he was going to tell me to drop my pants and lean over the bed so he could belt me, but he did no such thing. He looked at me with the most curious expression, and I thought he looked more sad and confused than angry.

I had the impression that he wanted to say something more to me but had no idea what or where to start. He looked like he couldn't even begin to form the words in his mind, much less say them, and for the first time in my life, I felt a surge of pity for my father. I assumed he was upset because he had such a failure for a son. I only understood much later, when he was sick and dying of cancer, that he had felt sorry for me because he understood the torment Bobby had put me through on a daily basis, and that he was actually glad that—finally—I had found the gumption to stand up to him and strike back.

"It's getting dark, so I'm not gonna send you out to work in the yard now, but as punishment, for the rest of the week, I want you to come home right after school and work on cleaning up the yard. You hear me?"

"What about Bobby? He should help."

My father looked at me but said nothing. His response was written on his face.

"Yes, sir," I said.

I was mad that Bobby wasn't being punished, too. After all, he had started it by making fun of me. But I was also relieved that my father had decided not to spank me. I couldn't help but wonder why. Later, I realized that this had been the tipping point in my growing up. What I had done had finally made it clear to my father that I wasn't a little kid any more, and he no longer needed to treat me like a misbehaving baby by spanking me.

"As for your brother…" my father said. He paused and, blinking his eyes rapidly, looked up at the ceiling. I couldn't believe it, but it looked like he was trying not to cry. "Stay away from him as much as you can, okay? Your squabbling drives both your mother and me crazy."

I nodded and said, "Sure thing." Apparently he didn't realize that I tried to avoid Bobby every minute of my life.

"Maybe when you guys get older you'll get along better than you do now. I certainly hope better than my brother and I got along, but for now… leave him alone, and let's hope he'll leave you alone."

"Okay."

"Maybe he learned his lesson."

My father was wrong about that, though. Bobby and I were never close, even as adults. Now that both of our parents are dead and gone, and he's a college professor out in Oregon, we never speak except on holidays and birthdays, and even then it's superficial.

"So…" My father held his hand out and beckoned me to come with him. "Mr. Wayrenen's still out in the front yard cleaning up that tree that came down. I want you to go over there and apologize to him like a man."

And that's exactly what I did. It wasn't as hard as I had thought. Walt even laughed and told me he was "impressed" by my "wallop." And then he said to my father: "You got a damned good kid there."

I was shocked when my father nodded and said, "I know."

If it wasn't for my concern about what had happened to Sylvia, I might have even been proud at that moment.

TWELVE

I had been relieved not to get whipped for beating up my brother and for punching Mr. Wayrenen, but the next day at school, I was distracted all day, thinking about Sylvia.

I was no longer wondering if she was real. The blood had been real for sure, but a part of me earnestly wished she *hadn't* been real so I could tell myself she wasn't lying out there in the beech tree clearing even now... that unless someone found her, she wasn't going to rot away, leaving me with nothing but memories.

By the end of the day, Mr. Ives threatened to call my parents. Every time he called on me, I got the answer wrong. Instead of reading during quiet time, I sat staring at the trees I could see outside the classroom window, wondering if any of them had young girls living inside them. I spent lunchtime alone instead of sitting with my friends. During recess, Jimmy asked me what was wrong. All I could say was that I wasn't feeling well.

That afternoon when I got home, my mother seemed sterner than usual as she directed me to go outside and get to work raking up leaves and picking up fallen branches. Even the prospect of a big fire to burn them didn't cheer me. I asked her why Bobby didn't have to help me, but she didn't answer. She just looked at me with "that look"... the one she gave me whenever I said something she thought was stupid.

I was exhausted from not sleeping well the night before and then dragging myself through school, so it took some effort to get motivated. After a while, though, with the sun warm on my back and a milder than usual breeze blowing into my face, I got into the rhythm of raking. As I worked, though, I couldn't stop from turning and looking across the backyard toward the woods.

I was nauseated by the thought that Sylvia's lifeless body would still be out there in the clearing, drained of blood from all those wounds that somehow... magically... had appeared on her body at the same time Walt was cutting down the Big Tree. I couldn't shake the feeling that even now, someone... if not Sylvia, then some other forest creatures were lingering at the margin of the woods and watching me.

Did they know Sylvia?

Were they aware that I had spoken to her?

Did they blame me for what had happened to her and the Big Tree?

Were they angry at me?

And would they want to get their revenge?

These and other questions filled my mind as I worked. As the afternoon drew to a close and daylight began to fade, I was suddenly filled with a desperate urge to go back to the beech tree clearing and find out if she was still there or, if she wasn't, if there was any evidence that she had ever been.

Long, blue shadows of trees stretched out across the lawn, and moisture glistened on leaves and branches, making it look like the world was coated with sparkling diamond dust. Angled bars of golden sunlight shot like spotlights through the branches that now blocked the setting sun. Like so many times before when I gazed from my bedroom window at the moon shining through the trees, I imagined these beams of light were roads that would lead me off into a fantasy world if only I had the courage and heart to walk them.

"Sylvia," I called out, my voice low and tight. The air had gotten chilly, and I shivered, saying her name. "I'm sorry... for what happened... There was nothing I could do."

I imagined or wished that my voice could somehow carry to her, wherever she was now even as I tried not to picture her lifeless body lying in a puddle of drying blood. Would she attract scavengers—crows and raccoons or skunks who would come and feast on her remains?

After a quick glance over my shoulder, I was satisfied that my mother and brother weren't watching me. Propping my rake against one of the birch trees, I set off across the backyard at an easy jog. I jumped the low stone wall that bordered our property and started across the field that led down a slope to the woods.

At the edge of the woods, I paused and looked back one last time. I saw my mother standing on the back porch, looking around, I assumed, for me. She appeared hazy, indistinct in the distance, and I wondered if she might be part of the dream world, not Sylvia. I watched her, but only for a moment. She cupped her hands to her mouth and called my name.

I didn't answer.

Instead, I turned and plunged into the darkening woods.

~ * ~

My feet made heavy drumming sounds on the ground as I ran. I knew exactly where I was going, but the winding trails took on a weird aspect the deeper I got into the woods. I stopped every now and then to get my bearings, unsure which way to go. Things looked different, somehow.

As I got deeper into the woods, the land sloped gradually down toward the swamp. The ground was still saturated from the storm, and the footing was less secure. A couple of times, my sneakers were almost sucked off my feet when I stepped into ankle-deep mud, but I kept on moving.

I was running... not like I was going *toward* something, but as if something was chasing after me. If my mother had seen me take off into the woods, I was sure she wouldn't come out here to fetch me. She might send Bobby, but I doubted it, so I consciously slowed my pace and focused on breathing evenly, telling myself there was nothing to be afraid of. Even though I have always been... well, not *afraid*, really, but on my guard. I was always cautious whenever I was in these woods... especially when it was getting dark. Over the years, I had imagined all sorts of horrors lurking here—jungle cats, bears and wolves, dinosaurs, ghosts, pirates, and wild Indians.

The day had been unusually warm, and I was sweating from working in the yard for a couple of hours without a break. Before long, my pant legs were soaked halfway up to the knees. A chill ran up my legs and back, and I had the distinct impression that it wasn't just from the dampness…

Someone I couldn't see was watching me.

Clutching, cold fear filled my chest when I got closer to the clearing.

What would I find when I got there?

I consciously slowed my pace as I became increasingly nervous. I didn't know which was worse to think about—that she *wouldn't* be there or that I would find her still lying face down on the trail, sliced to shreds and covered from head to toe with dried blood.

I desperately wished someone was there with me because either prospect brought a deep, gnawing fear.

For the first—and not the last—time in my life, I knew I was absolutely on my own.

What's the worst that can happen? I asked myself, but I didn't like the answer I came up with.

I could die.

The thought unnerved me, but then I thought that wouldn't be so bad after all.

I'd be dead, and I wouldn't care.

I wouldn't have to go to school anymore, and Bobby would finally stop beating up on me.

If I died, it might be a relief… unless I suffered before I died, or I came back as a ghost who haunted the woods and scared the crap out of Jimmy and my friends or anyone else who ventured out here.

Okay, so being dead wouldn't be so bad.

If that was the *worst*, what else could happen?

I might find Sylvia… dead.

That would be terrible because I would have to report what had happened. I couldn't just leave her out here for someone else to find. The police and adults and everyone would get involved trying to figure out who Sylvia was, where she came from, what she was doing out in the woods during and after the hurricane, and how she had come to be all cut up.

These and other thoughts crowded my mind so much that I arrived at the beech tree clearing before I realized it. I drew to a sudden halt and stared at the spot where I had last seen her. The sun was so low by now that the area was dense with shadows. I moved forward cautiously, my sneakers squishing with every step, but when I was about halfway there, I realized…

She wasn't there.

No body… no trace of blood… and—at least as far as I could see—nothing else to indicate she had ever been here.

I was stunned… and heartbroken.

This was the worst that could happen!

"Sylvia…?" I called out, my voice fail and fragile in the gloom.

I looked around, cocking my head to one side and listening… waiting for *any* response.

All I heard were the usual night sounds. It was too late in the season for frogs to be croaking in the swamp. They'd already settled deep in the mud for their winter hibernation. But the sounds of crickets and night birds filled the evening with faint music.

No voices.

"If you're out there…" I called out, but stopped. I had no idea how to finish, so I let my voice fade away.

What did I expect?

What did I *want* to happen?

Did I honestly think Sylvia was real and that she would suddenly appear to me, even though her tree—her home—had been destroyed?

Did I really think she might show up—if not now, maybe some night at the window and sit there on the roof so we could talk?

"This is stupid," I said, and then I heard—faint and far off—a voice, calling my name.

I jumped as a surge of panic filled my chest, but after a moment, I realized it was my mother. She must have guessed I had run off into the woods, and she was yelling my name as loud as she could. Her voice carried in the deepening darkness and, somehow, I found the strength to turn toward home. I cupped my hands to my mouth and yelled, "Coming!"

After one last, lingering look to make sure she really wasn't there, I turned around and headed for home.

THIRTEEN

"What were you doing out there?"
I squirmed in my seat and tried to look away, but my mother's steady stare unnerved me. My father was working late, and my mother, brother, and I had eaten a light supper. Throughout the meal, Bobby said next to nothing. I wondered if going nuts like I had and beating up on him had finally made him respect me, at least a little.

I doubted it.

Give him a couple of days... a week, tops, and he'd be right back at it.

"You were supposed to be working until your father came home."

"Even in the dark?"

"Don't you sass me."

I knew it wouldn't do any good to tell her I wasn't trying to be sassy.

"I—uh, I just wanted to take a break," I said.

I was still feeling keyed up from my walk in the woods because, although I hadn't seen or heard anyone—not even Sylvia—I was sure, now, that the whole time I was out there, someone… maybe *many* someones… had been watching me from the shelter of their trees. Now that I was safely home, my imagination took over, and I convinced myself that I had sensed them but hadn't dared admit it to myself because I didn't want to get scared.

I was sure, now, that there were forces or beings or whatever you want to call them out there in the woods. While they might not be outright evil, they certainly didn't seem to have my best interests in mind, either.

But Sylvia had been different.

She never would have hurt me.

She had been alone and afraid, and she needed shelter from the storm. She had been looking for safety after her home—The Big Tree—had been ripped apart by the hurricane.

I looked at my mother as she stood there in the kitchen doorway, waiting for my reply, but I had nothing. I stared at her helplessly, my mind a roaring blank, like the TV when the station goes off the air for the night.

Right then and there, I vowed that I would never go back into those woods… especially after nightfall… because I had no idea who or what might be waiting for me in the dark. I even determined that I'd be safer at night if I didn't sleep with the bedroom windows open, like I usually did, sometimes even in the winter.

I tried over the years to convince myself that I had made all this up, that none—not even Sylvia— was real.

How could she be?

Whatever the answer, I sure as heck didn't ever want to find out.

Still, for the rest of my childhood, late at night... usually in the summer months when it was so hot and humid I had no choice but to sleep with the bedroom windows open... while I hovered somewhere between wakefulness and sleep... I'd catch a faint voice calling to me from out of the darkness.

Whenever that happened, I was never sure if I was awake or asleep, dreaming, but I would suddenly jolt up in bed with a ragged intake of breath and find myself staring out of my bedroom window.

Usually, there would be nothing there but darkness broken by dappled moonlight, but if I looked hard enough over to where the Big Tree used to stand, I'd convince myself sometimes that I could see a small, indistinct figure of a girl. She would be wearing a flimsy, white nightgown, and she'd sit there in the moon-cast shadows of a tree I knew was no longer there, and she'd be staring up at me.

AFTERWORD

"The Big Tree" is what I would call a "typical" Rick Hautala story . . . but not in the pejorative sense. Not at all.

His novella contains all the elements of Rick's best work: clean, uncluttered prose; wistful nostalgia for a childhood none of us can ever recover; and a gentle braiding of all the narrative threads that leaves the reader satisfied, yet wanting the tale to somehow continue.

I think Rick's real talent was his ability to ratchet down the focusing tube of his microscope to the family level. A majority of his work examines the connective tissues that bind and sometime disjoint the basic social constructs of husbands, wives, fathers, mothers, and siblings. Throughout his career, he's shown an eerie awareness of the subtleties of the small stage—the family home and its inhabitants. "The Big Tree" gives us a look into the sensitive heart of a boy who so desperately needs an intimate relationship that he forms it with a favorite tree rather than a brother or friend.

The Big Tree knew all the narrator's secrets.

i

And that pretty much says it all.

About the story . . . but not about its creator. I was fortunate enough to know Rick Hautala not only through his work, but also through twenty years of friendship. We collaborated on screenplays, short stories, and even tried to create a TV series together. But that's not to say it was all sweetness and light—far from it. He and I had different philosophies on storytelling and *lots* of other things. I liked telling my stories on large, global stages with multiple viewpoints, and a variety of characters with a variety of voices; Rick much preferred his stories filtered through a single character's over-the-shoulder view of the world. He loved to explore the claustrophobic spaces of a single mind under stress and pushed to an extreme set of ultimate choices.

And that's when he would pull out some of his best surprises—because his characters often did not take the easy path, the one where no one's feelings (much less their kneecaps) get hurt. For as gentle and sensitive as Rick was in his world of friends and colleagues, he could exhibit a far less forgiving side in his stories of hidden secrets and debts to be paid.

I'm going to miss him and his endless energy and passion for writing. In the last few years, during our talks on the phone, he spoke with the same enthusiasm for every new book he started as the one he'd just finished. He turned out his pages grounded in the secure belief he was doing the work intended of him, the work for which he'd been made. I admired his determination and drive, and although I never told him, I drew a strength from his work ethic that inspired me to always keep writing the next page when sometimes, I saw little sense in it.

I think the body of a writer's work is something like Rick's Big Tree—within which the true spirit of the writer will always live. And the good thing is this: there is no hurricane big enough to ever blow it down.

And so, my friend, take Sylvia's hand and convince her of this simple truth.

—*Thomas F. Monteleone*
Fallston MD
4 June 2013

"I think, if anything, I'm a frustrated romantic who really does want to see the best of life, the positive aspects of people, but the world and nighttime prove me wrong all the time. The light casts shadows, and I've always been drawn to the shadows, the things at the edges of our awareness."

Rick Hautala
February 3rd, 1949 – March 21st, 2013

ABOUT THE AUTHOR

Rick Hautala has more than thirty published books to his credit, including the million copy, international best-seller *Nightstone*, as well as *Twilight Time*, *Little Brothers*, *Cold Whisper*, *Impulse*, and *The Wildman*. He has also published four novels—*The White Room*, *Looking Glass*, *Unbroken*, and *Follow*—using the pseudonym A. J. Matthews. His more than sixty published short stories have appeared in national and international anthologies and magazines. His short story collection *Bedbugs* was selected as one of the best horror books of the year in 2003.

He wrote the screenplays for several short films, including the multiple award-winning "The Ugly File," based on the short story by Ed Gorman, as well as "Peekers," based on a short story by Kealan Patrick Burke, and "Dead @ 17," based on the graphic novel by Josh Howard.

A graduate of the University of Maine in Orono with a Master of Art in English Literature (Renaissance and Medieval Literature), he served terms as Vice President and Trustee for the Horror Writers Association.

Rick Hautala died on March 21, 2013. His autobiography, *The Horror, The Horror*, was discovered by his wife Holly after his death and published in the summer of 2013.

His books *The Demon's Wife* and *Mockingbird Bay*, and his novel *Star Road*, written with Matthew J. Costello, were published posthumously.